The Siren and the Smoke Show

Leanne Alyse

Content Warning

This book is not appropriate for anyone under the age of eighteen! Reader discretion is advised.

If you would like to go in blind you can stop reading here. While this book is not dark romance like most of my oeuvre, there are still sensitive topics discussed as well as graphic sexual scenarios. I will still be giving a few content warnings.

Content Warnings: Handcuff play, light BDSM, cheating (off page, but heavily discussed)

This book is a work of fiction and is not based off real events. Any resemblance to people or events in real life is purely coincidental. Nor is this book meant to be an accurate representation of the real world. This is a fictional story, suspension of disbelief is recommended before opening these pages.

If you have any questions you can reach out to my email at <u>LeanneAlyseAuthor@gmail.com</u>.

And while this isn't a dark romance book please know that your mental health always matters <3

To the bisexual girlies who never actually got to date a woman because they married the gamer boy. I think I can help with that. ;)

LEANNE ALYSE

Playlist

Manchild – Sabrina Carpenter

As It Was – Harry Styles

Leave Me Alone – Renee Rapp

Boyfriend – Dove Cameron

Better Mistakes – Bebe Rexha

Redwine Supernova – Chappell Roan

Delicate – Taylor Swift

Make Out With Me – Maren Morris

"Slut!" – Taylor Swift

needy – Ariana Grande

Lie to Girls – Sabrina Carpenter

Death By A Thousand Cuts – Taylor Swift

Casual – Chappell Roan

Now That We Don't Talk – Taylor Swift

Moral of the Story – Ashe

Day One

"**A**llistine Lambert!" Kristen knocks on the door to my cabin. I cringe hearing my full ass government name. "Come on! It's our first full day on the boat! Do you really want to waste it locked in your room reading?"

Yes, but I'm not about to tell her that.

"I'll be there in a minute!" I promise, but I absolutely don't fucking mean it. I fully intend to spend the next half hour reading the new book that came out from my favorite author and occasionally scrolling on tiktok, thankful that I got the unlimited wifi.

"The show is at noon! You're going to miss it if you're still in your pajamas!" She calls. "Come on, you can't live in your kindle!"

I absolutely fucking can.

"I'll meet you down on deck five!" I call back through the door, but I don't get up off the bed.

The cabin is perfectly clean with its bleach white bedding or at least it was before I opened my suitcase and it all of the sudden looked like a bomb of clothing, hair products, and makeup went off. There is a small blue couch next to the bed with a desk across from it and a tiny coffee table in between the two. I'm honestly a little surprised they were able to fit so much stuff into such a small space.

I flop over onto my back with my kindle, my green eyes tracing over the words to a novella about a fireman who definitely doesn't do his job correctly. My hand runs over the bedding next to me but before I can let my mind drift to who was supposed to be there, I turn my attention out the window to the ocean.

We were picked up in Los Angeles. The cruise is two weeks and is going to take us to Hawaii and through the different islands.

The cruise that was supposed to be my honeymoon.

Kristen can say I'm moping all she wants. Her husband made it down the aisle. Mine made out with Missy Thompson. The asshole.

Who the fuck names a kid Missy? It's like when you name a dog Buddy cause you can't think of another name, but with a whole ass human being. I'm directing my anger at the wrong person, I know that, but Missy is still a bitch.

I take a deep breath and try to refocus my attention on the waves. They dance out on the horizon as far as the eye can see on every side. I've always loved the ocean. I was the one who wanted to go on the cruise so when I told Louis he was dead to me and that if I ever saw him again he would be dead to everyone else too, I made sure to also make it clear that I would be the one going on our honeymoon.

He seemed okay enough with that.

Another knock sounds outside my door exactly a half hour later like I knew it would and I actually get up this time. When I answer the door, Kristen pushes past me into the room, some of her perfectly blonde hair slapping me in the face as she does. Yellow sunflowers cover her light pink dress and her white sunglasses are perched on the top of her head.

"I told Kevin to fuck off to the casino for the day so we could spend it together." Kristen smiles, but it fades when she looks over me, "You're not dressed."

I glance down at my thin pajama shorts and the ratty t-shirt of Louis's that I stole as I was kicking him out. I sigh, running a hand through my light brown hair. "I–" Don't get a chance to get my excuse out because Kristen starts rifling through my suitcase that's sitting on the floor beside the bed.

She pulls out a very skimpy sundress that I'm one hundred percent sure she both bought and packed for me, and tosses it at my face. Light blue lace goes across the stomach almost making it look like a crop top and skirt, the top of it hanging off the shoulder with a deep v-neck and the bottom shorter than I'm comfortable with, but to be fair I don't love dresses that go above my knees.

I catch the dress with my fucking teeth, not on purpose, and grab it out of my mouth. "Can't I just wear leggings?" I grumble.

"Yeah right." Kristen huffs. "Get dressed. We're already late for the show."

I pull the t-shirt up and over my head, tossing it at the bed. We've been best friends since the day we were born so changing in front of each other isn't a big deal for us. I start putting on the dress. "Kris, the only thing that sounds worse than second acting The Little Mermaid at Sea, is sucking Louis's cock in my wedding dress."

"Would he be in the wedding dress or you be in the wedding dress?" Kristen clarifies.

I roll my eyes. "Does it really matter?"

She shrugs. "You set the parameters, I'm just making sure I understand them correctly."

I get the dress on and slip out of my shorts, I'm about to pull a pair of grannie panties out of my suitcase when Kristen tosses me a white thong that will absolutely be notice-able through this translucent dress. "Absolutely not."

"Okay, so you have two options." Kristen says, "You can either argue with me for twenty minutes about the panties and wear them anyways. Or, you could just put them on and I'll let you take your kindle to the bar instead of going to the musical."

I chew on my lip. "What's my third option?"

"There is no third option."

I grumble but slip on the white lace thong, that I'm also confident I didn't pack. "You said I can bring my kindle?"

"Yes." Kristen sighs. "If you must, but if you spend the whole time ignoring me, I'm going to confiscate it."

I chuck the kindle into my black handbag and toss it over my shoulder before slipping on my flats and gesturing out the door. "Let's just go. The sooner we get out of here the sooner I can be sipping margaritas in some lounge chair and day dreaming about hot firemen."

Kristen chuckles but heads out of the room. "I don't need one of those little boxes to day dream about hot firemen." She smirks.

I follow her through the hallways, the hard blue carpeting underfoot with runners lining the way to show where to go in case of an emergency. The hallways on the interior are plain with nothing but lots of doors spaced intermittently down them. When we get to the elevators there are a few other people loitering outside of them having quiet conversations.

A mother and her teenager, already complaining about being sea sick. A couple men in board shorts with very douchey looking hair cuts that remind me of Louis and a handful of women all laughing about something that I will never be privy too.

We are on the ninth floor which is almost entirely rooms. Kristen and Kevin's room is right next to mine since this was supposed to be a doubles honeymoon. We had booked it over a year ago and it wasn't long after that I found out about what happened with Missy. I tried to get my money back countless times but it was no use, teaches me not to book through a third party.

Kristen and I climb onto the elevator going down with a slew of other people since that's the one that she's leading me towards. "There's this cocktail lounge on the fourth floor that's supposed to have the best specialty drinks on the boat." She smiles as she slams on the button for four.

I shrug. "Whatever." I know it's been almost nine months since my fiance and I broke up, but that kinda shit sticks with you. Him and I started dating when we were freshmen in college and had been together ten fucking years before he threw it all away for a one night hook up.

I have the right to be mad for at least a year. What's the rule, one week for every month of the relationship? Ten years, twelve months in a year, that's one hundred twenty weeks I get to hate his guts. We're not even half way there.

The elevator stops a few different times to let other people off and on before getting to the fourth floor. Kristen drags my sorry ass out of the elevator the second the door opens and is pulling me down the hallway like she's a sled dog carrying a tree trunk. We should have gone to Alaska.

As she pulls me through the golden and blue halls of the ship we pass a few larger lounges, some gift shops, the casino which as we walk through, I hear Kevin cursing at one of the machines, likely losing the money everyone gifted them at their wedding. Eventually we get to a small lounge on the far end of the boat.

Kristen opens the door with a sign on the front that designates it as a smoking area, and the smell of the cigars invades my nostrils. She didn't mention that I would have to work through a cloud of smoke to get these drinks.

The room is all dark wood and darker leather. A long bar stretches all the way across the right side of the space. There are a handful of chairs at the bartop but no one is sitting there, everyone opting for one of the tables with black leather armchairs positioned in circles around them.

Kristen brings me over to one of the groups of seating that is near the notably closed window and I cough as I inhale the mass amounts of smoke we have to pass through.

I used to vape in college, but it's been years since I did any of that shit. It's clear to me though as Kristen pulls a dab pen out of her bag that she has different ideas from me of what will be fun on this trip.

I throw myself onto one of the large arm–chairs, sitting down on it crisscross and searching for my kindle in my bag before setting the bag down on the floor.

Kristen takes a longer drag than advisable of her dab pen before passing it over to me, but I push it away. "Oh come on, Alli. You know you want to." She taunts.

I chew on my lip as I look at the pink pen with the small capsule of light brown liquid on top. "I shouldn't."

Kristen seems like she was going to argue with me more but as a server comes over, she slips the pen back into her bag.

The woman's smile surprisingly seems to reach her eyes in a way it didn't with the rest of the people who I have seen working on the ship. "Hi!" The woman chirps, brushing some of the curly dark brown strands that were falling out of her bun away from her face. "My name is Kai, I'll be taking care of you." She passes us a couple drink menus. "I can give you a few minutes to hit that again and look over your options." She nods at Kristen's purse before turning and heading back away from us.

I roll my eyes at her a little. "Bitch."

Kristen slugs me on the shoulder. "Be nice. She didn't try to confiscate our dab pen, for that we owe her our lives."

"Yeah, and I'm the one being dramatic." I huff, as my eyes scan over the drink menu.

"Are you going to hit this now or what?" Kristen asked, taking another long puff before offering it to me again.

I sigh and grab it from her. "Give me that." I hiss. I put the dab pen to my lips and press down on the button inhaling deeply and holding it before breathing the smoke back out. I cough a little from not having taken a hit in something like six years before I toss it back at Kristen.

"Yay!" Kristen cheers, clapping her hands excitedly, "Maybe you'll be fun Alli for once instead of miserable Alli." She makes a pouting face as she says *miserable Alli* and slips the pen back into her purse.

We spend a couple minutes looking over the drink options on the menu that Kai handed us. These menus are specific to the Smoke Show Bar and Lounge but there is also a booklet on the table with things available everywhere on the ship.

The lounge has both food and drink which I found a little surprising. As I look around some of these people were so sunk into the chairs that I have a feeling they have been here since the place opened this morning. People, clearly high off their asses, snack on plates of fairly decent looking loaded fries and sip very colorful beverages and according to Kristen, today we will be joining their ranks.

It's fine. This is just for today and then to-morrow she will be back with her husband and I can spend the day how I want, laying out on my balcony and watching the waves with a bottle of wine from room service.

Kai comes back over again with a very large smile on her face. "Can I get you any-thing?"

Kristen bobs her head excitedly. "We'll both do a cool mint watermelon mojito," Wow, that sounds awful, "And two orders of your loaded fries."

"Got it, two mojitos, two loaded fries." Kai smiles.

"You seem very happy." Kristen smiles back at her.

"This is my last cruise before I head home." Kai chuckles, scribbling down our order on a note pad.

"Where's home for you?" Kristen asks.

I want to hiss at her to stop being so nosey, but Kai doesn't seem to mind.

"Hawaii." Kai tucks the notepad into her apron, "My family are Hawaiian natives. I thought working on a cruise line so close to home I would see them more but," She sighs, "Most of the stops don't tend to be very close to home."

"I'm sorry." I tell her. "That must be hard, being so close to home but not actually seeing your family."

She nods sadly. "Yeah. But I'll be home in two weeks." Her smile brightens again. "I'll go put in your orders."

My eyes trace over her ass as she walks away in a way that made me feel no better than a man, but to be honest, with how perfect the swell of her ass was, I have no regrets for staring. I do however regret that Kristen saw me.

The second that Kai was out of earshot she nodded after her. "You should totally go for it."

I scoffed. "I don't know what you mean."

"You totally do." Kristen argued. "And you never got your college lesbian phase because Louis chained you down at freshman orientation. You should ask for her number."

"We're on a cruise ship in the middle of the ocean," I tell Kristen, "We don't have cellular."

"Then her snapchat or something else." Kristen waves me off. "Just ask. What's the worst that can happen? She says no and we don't come back to this bar."

I'm still glaring at Kristen when Kai comes back with the drinks. "Thank you."

"Thank you." Kristen smiles. "Hey, my friend thinks you're really cute."

My eyes go wide. "Kristen." I hiss.

"Can she have your snapchat or pager number or however the hell you could communicate on the boat?" Kristen asks.

"I'm so sorry about her." I apologize.

Kai frowns a little, "So you don't want my snapchat then?" She asks, pulling out her notebook and a pen.

I chuckle a little and run a hand through my hair. "I..." I chew on my lip. "Yes. I... I would like your snapchat."

"Do you have a name?" Kai asked as she ripped off a piece of paper with her username on it and passed it to me.

"Alli." I respond, pulling on my phone and opening my snapchat. I add her username and the little icon that looks just like her comes up with the same beautiful curls and brown eyes.

She smiles. "Nice to meet you, Alli."

"Nice to meet you too, Kai."

Day Two

Kai sends me another snap of herself behind the bar pouring a drink with the caption, *"Wish you were here."*

I send back a picture off my balcony with the caption, *"I could say the same."* My green eyes watching the screen for the notification to go off again as I set the phone back down on the table beside me.

I finished the novella I was reading and started on another book, this one about a mafia man kidnapping an author and taking her to Europe. Vacation romance for my vacation felt very appropriate.

Kristen has in fact gone back to Kevin today and left me alone to my own devices and by devices I do mean my kindle. She and I had spent almost the entire day in the Smoke Show lounge, only leaving for a few hours to meet up with Kevin for dinner at which he told us proudly how he won two hundred dollars after wasting a thousand.

Idiot.

Whatever, it's Kristen's marriage, not mine and when she gets her first divorce, I'll make sure we go to Alaska for the divorce party.

My phone goes off again and I check it to see Kai has sent me another snap. It's a picture of her frowning with the caption, *"Now that's just mean, you know I'm stuck here. You have to cum here."* I have a feeling cum was spelled like that very deliberately.

I pull the phone back and send her a picture of my bikini. *"Can't, this isn't exactly Smoke Show appropriate attire."*

Her reply is instant; it's a picture of her smirking with the caption, *"I'd love to see what's underneath."*

I chew on my lip for a second before sending a picture of my legs, *"You first."*

I stare at the little icon for a solid minute waiting for her to open it, but the arrow stays solid. I set my phone down and chuckle to myself. I'm being crazy. She's not going to send a picture of her tits... right?

Maybe Kristen is right, I did miss my college lesbian phase, and it seems like I'm trying to make up for it right now.

I open back up my kindle and start to read, trying to distract myself from Kai and the snap that she still hasn't fucking opened a solid half hour later. Yes, I do keep fucking checking even though I absolutely should not be. In my defense, it's really hard to read about this mafia dude railing this innocent chick when all I can fucking do it wait for Kai to snap me back.

It takes an hour, a whole fucking hour, but eventually she does open the snap and then goes quiet again.

I hear Kristen open the door to the balcony next to mine and she sticks her head out. "Hey! I've been knocking on your door for like five minutes."

"You really shouldn't do that." I tell her as I set my kindle down and move to head back inside. I open the door to my room and Kristen was already standing on the other side of it. "I had the door closed so I didn't hear you."

She hums. "Excuses." Kristen pushes inside and collapses onto my bed. "Kevin is pissing me off, so I told him to go find one of the many bars on the ship and waste his time there. Wanna go back to the Smoke Show and see your girlfriend?"

I roll my eyes. "She's not my girlfriend." I hold up my phone. "Hell she's not even messaging me back." But as though the universe wants to prove me wrong my phone goes off.

"Is that her?" Kristen jumps excitedly and snatches my phone out of my hand. She knows my passcode and unlocks it before I can even say anything.

"Don't!" I try to grab the phone back but it's too late, Kristen is already opening the snap.

Kristen gasps as she flips the phone around for me to see. It's a picture of Kai in what seems to be a walk in freezer with her tits out, her nipples hard likely from the cold as her breath fogs over her body. "She seems like she's messaging you back to me."

I stare at the photo a second longer and the beautiful pink puckered nipples. Fuck, I want to lick her.

The caption reads, *"Your turn."*

I grab the phone back away from Kristen and exit out of the snap. "I can explain that." I assure her, even though I have no fucking idea how the hell I'm going to explain that.

Kristen calls my bluff. "I'd like to see you try." She chuckles.

When I just kinda stare between her and the phone she knows she has me caught. In the end I just say, "Can you get out so I can send her a picture back?"

Kristen shrugs. "Fine but then get dressed. We're heading back down there." Luckily, she does actually leave the room after that.

I get back to where I was sitting on the balcony and send her a picture of me with my bikini top on. *"Don't let your coworkers see the next one."* Then I shimmy my bikini top down and send her a picture with it off.

I close my phone and immediately feel like I made a bad decision. I've never sent a nude in my fucking life and now I'm snapping some random chick I met yesterday my tits? What if she screenshots them? My breasts aren't as big as hers, what if she didn't like them?

This was such a bad idea.

I see her open the snaps and there is no indicator that they were screen shot so I feel a shred of relief flood me because of that but I'm still anxious as all hell to actually go see her now.

Another snap comes through, the picture is taken from under the bar of her smiling down at the phone, *"Your body is beautiful."* There's a second snap after it. *"I'd love to see more of it."* This one is a picture of the well behind the bar.

I don't respond, since I'm going to be there in roughly fifteen minutes anyways. I bring my kindle back inside and toss it into my handbag again.

Rifling through my suitcase, I try to find something even slightly as cute as the dress I wore yesterday, but it's a tall order and I can't just wear that dress again, that would be weird, I'd feel like a cartoon character. After a minute of searching through my bag I bang on the wall between mine and Kristen's room and there's a knock at the door a second later.

"What?" She grumbles.

"Help me, my wardrobe sucks." I plead.

Kristen scoffs. "I've been telling you that for years." She pushes me aside and starts tearing my suitcase apart even more than it already was, humming at different options and sighing at others. She pulls out my ripped leggings and a loose tie dye blue tank top with lace straps. "Wear this. It's ugly, but it's you and if you're going to dress like shit you should at least dress like yourself."

I grab the tank top and pull it over my head, not bothering with a bra since I'm already wearing a bikini. I pull on the ripped leggings and go to look in the mirror. Yeah, not as hot as what I wore yesterday, but definitely myself this time and that has to count for something.

I pull my hair up into a messy bun since it's starting to get blazing hot on this boat and free a few of my smaller strands along with my bangs. I turn to Kristen. "Good?"

She shrugs. "For you? Great. Now let's go."

I chuckle at Kristen as she balances the empty drink glass on her head, teetering and tottering back and forth to keep it upright.

Kai comes by and snatches it, setting it back down on the table, "Come on, ladies, I thought we were friends. I don't want to have to clean up broken glass today and send Kris to the medic."

"Sorry, Kai." Kristen and I mutter in tandem.

Kai shrugs. "It's fine, honestly it was a little impressive."

"I've been doing that trick since college." Kristen says proudly, grabbing the glass and sipping at the straw for any last remanence of watermelon mint mojito in the glass even though it's basically all ice.

"Another?" Kai asks.

Kristen nods. "Yes, please."

Kai turns to me with a smile. "Wanna see how I make them?"

I look nervously between her and the bartop. "Am I allowed back there?"

"Nope." Kai chuckles. "But Beau is on his fifteen and everyone else is in the kitchen. No one will see." Kai grabs my hand and pulls my high ass up to my feet before dragging me across the room.

I follow blindly, a part of me feeling like I'm getting away with something as she leads me behind the bar. I glance around, paranoia from the weed seeping into me as I worry that someone might come by and yell at us, but the bar is pretty empty today and none of the patrons really look like they care.

Kai drops my hand once we are at the well and she gestures widely with her arms. "Welcome to my lair." She smirks.

"I love what you've done with the place." I smile at her, admiring the many rows of bottles that I could barely see from over where I was sitting before. There is so much fucking alcohol back here, all blocked with small golden railings so it doesn't fall is the ship moves too much.

Kai gestures to the well, "Most of the regulars here like the well. They tend to be more concerned with the other end of the place." She nods to the walk in humidor on the opposite side of the room. "But for the fancier drinkers like yourself we have things like this." She pulls out a bottle of watermelon Malibu.

She grabs two glasses and pours a shot into each, not bothering to use the measuring glass as she does. She picks up a couple of mint leaves from her garnish tray and rolls them in her hands before tossing them into the drinks. "I don't bother muddling them even though we're supposed to, I've never been able to tell the difference so I assume no one else can either." She shrugs.

I chuckle a little and play with the light brown strands falling out of my bun, still not sure how to talk to her. It's so much easier when we're chatting on snap. I can't explain it but I'm just better at communicating with people through my phone. In person... yeah, the pretty girl is gonna make me nervous as all hell.

"Wanna use the soda gun?" She asks as she shovels some ice into the glasses.

I chew on my lip. "I've never used one before." I tell her as she lifts it from its holder and passes it to me. I hold the thing timidly and far away from myself like I'm scared it's going to fucking bite me or some shit.

Kai points at one of the buttons labeled *SODA*. "Hold the gun over the drinks and press that one."

I do as instructed and the glasses fill with soda water until Kai tells me to stop.

"Very good." She smiles, her hand coming to rest on my back just below my shoulder as she rubs it softly. She takes the soda gun back from me and puts it back in its holder. "Next I'll teach you how to take orders and run food, then finally I'll have good help instead of Beau." She chuckles.

I smile back at her as she moves her hand down lower on my back. I turn to her and our eyes fix on each other.

She smirks a little as she pushes some of the hair away from my face with the hand that's not resting on the small on my back. She pulls me in a little closer and I can feel her breath gracing against my lips.

We're about the same height but somehow she feels taller like she's towering over me even though it's maybe only an inch. I feel so fucking intimidated right now in a way I've never felt when I was seconds away from kissing a guy.

My heart is racing out of my chest and I'm sure it's going to fucking explode as the soft scent of her sweet perfume wafts over me. For a moment it feels as though I'm frozen in time, trapped between two moments and a choice to run or to let this happen.

But in the end, that choice doesn't find me because the door to the kitchen opens. "Hey!" Beau calls. "You can't be behind the bar."

My hands go up immediately, "Sorry!" I apologize before scurrying out of Kai's arms and away from behind the bar. My chicken shit ass regretting that I didn't just fucking kiss her when I had the chance.

Day Three

I'm getting so sick of being stuck on this stupid boat. Maybe I'm just salty because Kai hasn't snapped me since that thing happened behind the bar. Her and Beau got in an argument and then Kai went home early, flipping him off as she headed through the door to the back. She was really fucking pissed.

I should snap her but I've been scared that if I snap her and she doesn't snap back that it means she really doesn't want to talk to me. At least if I don't send her anything I can delude myself into believing that she's waiting for me to say something first.

Most of today has been spent in my room because Kristen and Kevin actually have been able to stand each other, surprisingly. I've thrown up more than twice already because I'm so sea sick from being on a boat for three days straight. I'm so ready to see land but we won't actually dock until day six.

Why did I think this cruise was going to be a good idea?

I really can't remember right about now.

My phone goes off and I jump for it on my bed having just come out of the bathroom from what is now my third time throwing up. I want it to be Kai, but it's not.

It's Louis.

I've been trying to get myself to block him on socials since we broke up but... yeah, it's a lot easier said than done. I've changed my relationship status, I've unfriended and unfollowed him on most things, but actively blocking him? Yeah, I don't know if I can do that.

Ten years of my life, years of waiting for him to finally pop the question, years of building a life together, all just gone over one stupid mistake.

He's apologized countless times, but I know it goes deeper than just the cheating. We were having problems before that. We've been having problems for years. We just kept burying them until they were too big and he finally did something drastic.

I stare down at the notification, knowing full well I shouldn't open it. I should delete it. This isn't the first time he's snapped me and every time I tell myself I'm not going to open it, I tell myself I'm going to finally block him, but every time I find my finger hovering over the little red square and pressing down.

The snap opens and it's a picture of him, his shaggy red hair in messy short curls around his face and his eyes a slightly deeper green than mine staring at the camera like he wants to fuck it, oh yeah, and he's not wearing a fucking shirt. *"Just checking if you're still mad at me. I miss you, Liss."*

I glare at the damned thing but I don't close it, my eyes tracing over his abs and getting stuck on where the screen cuts off. I can't tell if he's wearing pants or not with the angle but I want to find out.

No.

No, lizard brain. We aren't fucking doing that. Asshole. He's an asshole who can rot in hell. I click the screen to exit out of the picture and toss my phone across the bed. "Rot in hell." I growl at it more than him, mad at the phone for not holding the image of him anymore.

I take a deep breath and try to remind myself that I'm better off, that I'm giving myself an opportunity to find myself and all that other bullshit people say to themselves after a break up to make themselves feel better. None of it's working.

But then my phone goes off again.

I grumble and throw myself face first onto the bed with a scream, trying to remind myself to have self control and not to open whatever it was that Louis was probably sending me.

I make it about two minutes, I'm assuming because I have no way of knowing for sure, before I pick up the phone again, but instead of Louis's name next to the snapchat notification, it's Kai's with the beautiful flower after her name.

I open that a hell of a lot faster, skipping the humming and hawing that I had with Louis's snap.

Kai wasn't behind the bar like I expected her to be, she was sitting on a bed crisscross with the camera angle taken down over top of her. Instead of the white button up and black slacks she wore when she was working, she was in a pair of white shorts and a plain light blue v-neck. *"I'm off today."*

That's all the snap reads. I pace back and forth debating if she's looking for an invite to hang out or not. Do I really want to hang out with her after I've been throwing up all morning? I feel disgusting.

I close my phone and go brush my teeth no less than five times before finding the Dramamine in my makeup case and popping some. Once I'm sure that I can actually see straight and won't puke on Kai, I make my way over to the outside of my cabin and take a picture of my number, making sure to keep the door open so I don't lock myself out.

I send her the picture with the caption, *"Need something to do?"* Then I head back into my room.

Her reply is almost instant, a picture of her in the hallways with a huge smile on her face. *"I think I just found something to do... or someone maybe."* There's a winking emoji after it.

I chuckle and I'm about to toss my phone on the bed, when I notice that my room still has clothes all the fuck over the place in random piles. This place is a disaster.

Without really considering what's clean or dirty or what I'm doing, I start throwing absolutely everything I see in my suitcase with the mentality of, I'll sort it all out later when the hot bartender is not coming up the elevator.

I miss the suitcase with about half the clothing I throw into it and find myself on the floor trying to push everything inside when there's a knock on the door outside. "Oh shit." I whisper, popping up to my feet just a little too fast and feeling the nausea roll through my stomach and the dizziness flutter through my head.

I look around and the place is slightly more organized than it was when I started but not by a lot. Whatever, it's the best I'm going to get.

I intentionally slow my steps as I walk towards the door, forcing myself to take a deep breath so I don't completely lose my stomach, my mind, or whatever fucking else before I let my hand rest on the handle.

She's just a woman.

It's not like I'm a virgin or some shit, I've just never been with a woman. The experience can't possibly be that different from being with a man and I don't even know if we are going to do anything or just hang out. I'm getting ahead of myself and over thinking it, I just need to open the fucking door and–

Another knock.

"Alli?" Kai's voice lilts through the door before muttering. "I swear to god if she sent me a fake room number I'm going to be so embarrassed."

I turn the handle. "Hi." I whisper.

She smiles. "Hi." She replies.

We stare at each other on opposite sides of the doorway for a moment before she runs a tawny hand through her dark brown curls. Every other time I've seen her it's been up in a bun so seeing now how her hair goes all the way down her back feels strangely personal.

"Are you going to invite me in?" Kai asks sweetly.

I nod and move to the side of the door, "Yeah, come in." I chew on my lip trying to work through the nerves that are eating a hole in my stomach.

Kai smiles as she breezes past me into the room and her perfume wafts over me. She smells fucking divine in a way that I'm surprised I hadn't noticed until I got this close to her.

I close the door softly, wanting to make sure it doesn't slam like it was prone to do when I just let it go. When I make my way into the main part of the room, Kai is already lounged out on the couch, her eyes watching the ocean as we cruise by.

"Beautiful, isn't it?" She purrs. "I've always loved the water."

I don't know where to sit. Is it too forward to sit next to her on the couch? Should I be putting some distance between us in case she doesn't want anything more than to chat? Should I just take the bed or is the bed worse because then I'm implying I want to be on the bed?

Oh fuck, she's staring at me.

She asked me a question. What was the question?

Okay, just nod.

Kai chuckles a little. "You seem nervous." She pats beside her on the couch like it's her room, "Come sit down."

Okay, well at least that answers the question on where to sit. I move across the room and sit beside her on the couch and she tosses her legs over me before grabbing my hands and interlocking them with her own.

I relax, for like half a second, before I realize she just made it very fucking clear that this is going to be more than just talking and I have no idea what the absolute fuck I am doing.

"We don't have to do anything if you don't want to." She says. "I can tell you're nervous, I just..." She pulls her hands away and moves her legs. "I thought maybe you liked me."

"I do." I whisper. "I just... I've never done this before."

"Kissed someone?" She asks.

I shake my head. "I've only ever been with men."

"But you do know how to kiss someone?" She clarifies and I nod. "I mean, maybe not well since you've only ever batted for the wrong team, but I promise kissing a woman is the same principle as kissing a man."

"I kiss just fine." I mutter.

Kai shrugs. "I'd like to see you prove it."

I see what she's doing, but as my eyes look into hers, I quickly find myself responding to the dare. I lean forwards awkwardly, not touching any of her but just hovering over her body. Kai is already laughing before

I even get close to her lips like she thinks this is the funniest thing in the entire fucking world. She puts a hand on my face and pushes me back. "Oh, you don't kiss a woman like that."

I grimace.

She stands up off the couch. "Here, let me show you." Kai climbs on top of me, straddling my lap as she sits on my thighs. She runs her hands through my hair as she tilts my head up to look at her. Then slowly, painstakingly slowly, she lowers her lips down to mine.

Her lips are softer than anyone I've kissed in the past. She doesn't immediately invade my mouth with her tongue like I'm used to with Louis, instead she sucks my lower lip into her mouth and bites down on it gently with her teeth.

I gasp a little at the bite before her tongue starts to lick at the ache she caused. I moan a little as her mouth finally opens and our tongues begin to dance softly around each other.

Kai grabs my hands with hers and she places them on her hips. "Touch me." She whispers.

I nod and let my hands run down her sides to the swell of her ass. Her beautiful fucking ass. My hands stay over her clothing to be respectful, but I do grab pretty fucking hard. I want to smack her ass, but I have no idea if that will be too much or not.

Kai grinds on top of me, her hands playing in my hair as she and I continue to kiss. She rakes her hands through the strands as she uses the hair to keep my head backwards.

After a few moments like this she pulls away, both of us breathless as she leans down and whispers into my ear, "How far do you want to go?"

I chew on my lip. "I... I don't know."

"If you don't know, then we should stop." Kai climbs off of me and I try to remember that she's doing this to make me feel more comfortable so it's not fair for me to be upset that her body is leaving mine. "We can just talk today. I'm off until we get into port, there's always tomorrow."

I nod and smile as I scoot down the couch to make some room between the two of us. "Yeah." There's always tomorrow.

Day Four

"**I** couldn't believe he drank that many!" Kai smiles as she sits on the edge of the bed across from where I'm propped up against the headboard. "He was one of the wilder people to come into the Smoke Show during my time here."

I chuckle as I run my hand over the bedding. "Old fashions are not good enough to warrant drinking ten of them in a day."

"He spaced them out enough and didn't seem all that drunk so I couldn't turn him away!" She laughs just about doubling over. "I couldn't believe it either though. I thought for sure by the end of the day I would need to send him to the medic, but he was fine."

I smile at her. "You must have a million good stories."

Kai hums. "Some, but not as many as you'd think. Most days it's just like any other bar. Only difference is this one moves." She puts her hand in the air and lets it slowly glide forwards.

"And it has one hell of a view." I smile, looking out the window. "The ocean is gorgeous."

"I've always seen the ocean at the bars I've worked at." She shrugs. "Most of them were on the beaches in Hawaii. The sunset over the water is one of the most beautiful things I've ever seen."

"I've never been before." I tell her softly.

"You will have in a few days." She smiles but then her smile turns a little sad.

"What's wrong?" I ask her softly.

Kai shakes her head. "Nothing." She says.

I don't know if I should push or just let it go. If she doesn't want to talk about it, I already gave her the option to. I don't want to be too invasive. "Okay." I whisper.

There is a silence that passes through the room as both of us turn our attention to out the windows of the balcony. We watch the water pass us by as the sun begins to set outside on the horizon. The sky is alight with oranges and pinks and purples, with clouds hovering out in the distance distorting the colors.

Kai scoots up next to me on the bed so we are both against the headboard. She leans her head on my shoulder and wraps an arm around me.

I lean back into her and my hand drifts down to her thigh.

She smiles at me. "Did you want to kiss again?"

I nod. "Yes."

She grabs me by the shoulders and positions me down on the bed so I'm laying the wrong way across it with my head tilted over the side to look out the windows. "There, now we can both see the ocean."

I chuckle as she presses her lips down to mine and I can in fact see the sun setting over both of us. Her lips taste like strawberries and she's honestly more beautiful than the fucking sunset. I'd rather be staring at her.

Kai's hands rove down my body this time, finding the underside of my crop top and pausing briefly at the hem. She pulls back from my lips for a second, "Can I?"

"Yes." I whisper. I grab her and pull her face back down to mine, needing to taste her strawberry lip gloss again.

Her hands slip under the crop top with a painstaking slowness that has me squirming underneath of her. She lifts my sports bra and positions it above my tits as she begins to kiss down to my neck. Her lips lock around the soft flesh there and she starts to suck hard. She palms the swell of my breast and her thumb starts to massage over my nipple at the same time she's leaving the hickey.

I moan, my eyes trained on the sunset behind me. I force myself to slow down, force myself to take in this moment and remember every fucking second of it.

Remember Kai on top of me.

Remember the smell of her sweet perfume.

Remember the way her thumb feels on my nipple.

Remember the way her lips feel on my neck.

Remember the way her hair flows over her back.

Remember it all because suddenly the realization that Kai had earlier slams into me like a ton of fucking bricks.

This. Won't. Last.

Fuck.

How have I not thought about that?

At the end of next week I'll be heading back to Utah with a tan and a great story and she'll be back home in Hawaii with her family. It's a seven hour flight and thousands of dollars for either of us to ever see the other. There's no happy ending here. Best case scenario we snap for a little while before we eventually forget the other exists.

I take a deep breath and remind myself that dreading the future will just take away from the present. I need to enjoy the time I do have with her.

She can see my mind is drifting. Kai pulls away from my neck with her lips and tilts my head up towards her. "Hey, focus on now." She whispers like she could tell exactly where my mind went.

I nod, but I don't feel like I mean it. "Okay." I whisper back anyways.

Kai's lips go back to my neck as she murmurs against it, "What do you think Kristen will say when she sees the hickeys?" She chuckles.

I chuckle back. "Oh, she'll have a lot to say."

She kisses my neck. "Let's make sure of that then." Kai bites down on the soft flesh there and begins to suck again, but instead of her hand staying on my breasts, she starts to drift down my body. Her fingers play in the hem of my leggings as she bites down again and I can tell she's waiting for permission.

"Yes." I breathe out.

Kai doesn't hesitate before slipping her hand underneath the leggings and between my legs. She finds my center instantly and her fingers start massaging at my clit somehow knowing exactly how to fucking work me.

"Fuck." I cry out, my head tilting back as I groan which doesn't feel sexy in the slightest until Kai is humming into my neck.

She pulls her lips away and I can feel the heat from where she left the hickey. I want to reach up and touch it, but I want to touch her more.

My hands find her hips as she continues to play with my clit and she nods feverishly when my hands fist in her shirt. I pull the shirt up and over her head and the way her breasts glow in the setting sun is a sight I will never fucking forget as long as I live.

She isn't wearing a bra and somehow that doesn't feel presumptuous as much as it feels confident; like she knows where this is going and she's ready for it. Kai smiles as my hands find her tits and my thumbs flick over her nipples. She grinds on top of me as she moves her fingers and I find myself approaching the edge as quickly as if I had done it myself.

I moan as I chew on my lip trying to calm myself down so I don't just finish on the spot, but, "I'm so fucking close." She's fucking amazing at this. It's clear she knows what she's doing and isn't afraid to show it.

Kai slips her fingers between my pussy lips and continues to work me with her thumb, "Finish on my fingers." She orders softly.

I nod and stop trying to fight it. My orgasm washes over me in beautiful waves like the ones outside the boat, cresting over me in pulses as she continues her soft motions. My whole body releases every ounce of tension I felt earlier as I try my best to breathe through one of the best orgasms of my fucking life.

"Kai." I moan.

"Alli." She smiles back.

I sit upright and she leans back a little to allow me to do so. I prop myself upright with my hands behind my back as my lips press back to hers. She swirls her tongue around mine as she continues to grind onto my lap.

I need to repay the favor, but I have no idea how to touch a woman other than myself. I take a deep breath and try to remind myself that, worst case scenario, I have a wand in my bag that I'm absolutely sure I can figure out how to use on someone else and do my best to gently grab her waist and flip her onto her back.

Kai giggles as she lands on the bed beside me and scoots so her head is hanging over the edge and she's staring out at the now darker sky. The lights inside aren't on so we can still see some of the light streaking up into the sky even though the sun is mostly down. She smiles at the sky or at the water or at me, I'm not sure but she has a beautiful fucking smile.

I climb between her legs and pull her shorts down while she hums excitedly. My hand slips between her legs and I start to make small circles around her clit with my index and middle fingers. I rub softly, like I'm scared I'm going to hurt her, but when she doesn't make a sound, I know I'm not applying enough pressure. I push down a little harder and try to remind myself of what I like when I do this on myself.

She moans then and I smile feeling very accomplished, even just after that small sound that slipped past her lips. I want to make her moan again.

I press down and make sure to avoid scratching her with my nails, using the balls of my fingers to keep her stimulated.

She nods happily and purrs, "Keep going. You're doing good."

The encouragement helps more than I think she will ever fucking know, but I feel a little more steady in myself as I continue to rub circles around her clit. I make sure not to speed up too much or vary anything I'm doing in some crazy way. She said it's good, I want to stick with good.

Kai moans again and I take a deep breath trying not to show that my heart is absolutely thumping right out of my chest. I feel like it's going to fucking explode. Why is giving so much more nerve wracking than receiving?

I need to give the guys of my past more credit for even bothering to try. I had no idea it was this terrifying fingering a woman.

Focus.

Somehow, even with all my mental blathering, I keep my pace steady and I'm able to bring Kai to the edge. She starts bucking under my hand and I struggle a little more then to keep up the stimulation, but I manage.

"Fuck, Alli!" She cries out as she finishes, her clit throbbing as tremors wrack through her body. After a moment she stops shaking and I pull my hand away.

Kai rolls over onto her side, panting heavily as she smiles up at me. "For your first time," She pants out, "You did great."

I smile a little, feeling beyond satisfied with myself as I collapse down onto the bed next to her and Kai pulls me into her arms. "Maybe next time we can try oral." I whisper.

She chuckles. "Maybe next time we can try handcuffs."

Day Five

Kai pours a crap ton of cream and sugar into her cup before filling it with coffee from the carafe. She takes her coffee and a chocolate pastry from the tray before leaning back into me on the couch. It's her second cup and my third but the cups are small, so we haven't kicked the pot yet.

We ordered room service for breakfast and last night for dinner. She spent the night in my room, talking until the odd hours of the night and then... not talking some more. I don't think we actually fell asleep until it was five and when the breakfast got here, I stumbled out of bed trying to get it, still exhausted from being so sleep deprived, but if I went back, I would do it all over again.

Kai looks at my coffee and sighs.

"What?" I ask, confused.

She shrugs. "I just think life is too short for black coffee."

My brows furrow a little. "It's not like I only drink black coffee." I counter, "I just like it in the mornings because the bitter taste helps to wake me up."

"You know what else helps you to wake up?" Kai waves her cup in the air, "Caffeine."

"Yeah, okay." I mutter, "But I still don't mind the taste of black coffee. I'm not like a purest or anything, I just think that it gets a bad rep."

Kai scoffs. "It gets the reputation it deserves. Black coffee should be a sin. It needs cream. You wouldn't eat toast without butter. It needs a companion."

"I like jam with my toast." I whisper like this is awkward before breaking out into a laugh.

She looks at me like I'm being ridiculous. "Do you not put butter with the jam?" She asks.

I shake my head. "No." I run a hand through the rat's nest of my hair. I haven't brushed it since I woke up and I'm sure it's a fluffy mess, likely sticking up in weird ways that I don't intend for it to.

Kai moves off of me and smiles. "What a coincidence that it's breakfast and we have jam, butter, and toast!" She slathers a piece with more butter than I would find advisable and then holds up the little packets of jam. "Grape or strawberry?"

"Strawberry, I don't like grape." I answer.

She makes a sad face. "We need to expand your palate." She says, but she takes the strawberry jam regardless and spreads the whole thing over the toast before passing it to me. "Here, try with butter."

I chuckle and take the piece from her. I take a bite and chew. It has the profile of the jelly that I'm used to but there's a creaminess to it that the butter adds. "Admittedly, this is better than how I usually have it."

Kai gestures emphatically. "See! I told you." She passes me her cup of coffee. "Now try this."

I take the cup from her and sip softly at it with a chuckle. The bitterness is softened by the sugar and the cream in a way that reminds me of when I get flavored coffees.

"Good right?" She asks.

I chuckle. "Yes, it's good." I pass her the cup back.

She takes it and sets it down before taking mine from me too. She pours creamer and sugar into my already mostly full cup and stirs it with a spoon somehow managing not to splash any over the edge then passes it back to me. "There, better."

I roll my eyes a little but take the coffee anyways, running a hand through my hair again as I do. "You are one of those people who always believes they can fix everyone, aren't you?"

Kai shrugs. "I *can* fix everyone." She counters before taking another bite of her pastry.

"You know you don't have to, right?" I whisper, brushing some of the hair away from her eyes. "You don't need to always make everything right."

Kai chuckles a little nervously. "If I don't, no one else will." She smiles sadly in that way that doesn't reach her eyes.

"Maybe people will fix their own problems." I suggest softly.

She shakes her head. "No, my family isn't like that and my work life has never been that either. I have to take matters into my own hands or nothing will ever get done."

"That's a lot to put on yourself." I tell her, looking at her softly.

She scoffs a little. "Like you're any different?" She challenges.

"How do you mean?" I ask.

"I've seen you and Kristen at the Smoke Show." Kai says, "You're always two drinks behind her if not more. You take one hit of the dab pen to satisfy her but beyond that you stay mostly sober."

I chew on my lip. "Kristen just needs someone to look out for her."

"And if not you then no one else will." Kai supplies, "So don't act like you don't do the same thing I do."

I hold my hands up in surrender. "You're right."

She smiles. "I usually am."

A soft silence passes through the room and even if our conversation was a little tense the silence doesn't feel that way.

Kai snuggles back into me and we turn our attention out towards the waves again, "I go back to work tomorrow." She huffs.

"I have excursions that I already paid for and Kristen is going to expect me to go on." I grumble.

"Oh, poor you." She rolls her eyes. "You have to go have fun snorkeling in Hawaii. I'm going to have to deal with Mrs. and Mr. too cheap to leave the boat." I knew who she was talking about instantly.

"We're actually going parasailing." I mutter.

She shudders. "Ooh, heights. That's not fun."

I nod sheepishly. "Plus, I'll be stuck in the air for like an hour with Kevin."

"Yeah..." She trails off stretching out the word. "I haven't even met him yet. Is he around much?"

I shrug. "Not really."

Kai nods. "My sister's husband is like that."

"You have a sister?" I ask.

"I have three sisters," Kai answers, "I'm the youngest of six."

"Holy crap, that's a big family." I take a sip of my coffee, now with cream and sugar. "I'm an only child. But I've known Kristen my whole life, she's like a sister."

Kai chuckles. "There's nothing quite like a sister." She says. "There's something about sharing parents that just creates a different kind of bond than with a best friend. That's not to diminish yours and Kristen's relationship, but in my experience, it's not the same."

I frown a little, but don't argue with her on it. I'd rather not spend whatever time her and I have together fighting or worse, scare her away. So instead of trying to explain to her that just because we didn't share parents doesn't mean Kristen and I aren't basically sisters or how I spent most nights at Kristen's house growing up because my dad wasn't around and my mom was working, I just change the subject.

"We should have ordered more of those pastries." I nod to the half empty plate of them. "We destroyed those." I chuckle.

Kai nods. "There's always next week. I have four days on and then three more off." She tilts her head to look at me and smiles as she presses a kiss to my lips.

"That sounds nice."

Day Six

"**Y**ou've been spending a lot of time with Kai." Kristen smirks as we stand in line to get off the boat. "And... are those hickeys on the back of your neck?" She chuckles.

I grumble and pull my hair out of the claw clip even though it's hot as hell. "I knew I should have just worn my hair down." I mutter.

Kristen hums. "So I take it things have gotten serious." She surmises. "How's it being with a woman?"

"Kristen." I hiss like I'm worried someone is going to hear her, but Kevin has his earbuds in, only barely covered by his shaggy brown hair, and isn't paying a lick of attention to what either of us are saying. We could probably scream *Alli's a fucking lesbian* in his face and he wouldn't even notice.

I sigh. "Yeah, we hook up, but no, it's not serious."

Kristen scrunches her brows confused. "Why not?" She asks as we pass down the gang plank and onto the island.

"Because there's no future there." I whisper sadly. "She lives in Hawaii and that's roughly three thousand miles away from Utah."

"You looked it up?" Kristen asked.

"I was curious." I shrug. "But regardless, she's got her life and I've got mine. There's no world where I'm going to up and move to Hawaii or she's going to move to Utah. She already has been talking about how much she misses her family just having been apart from them for the past year while she's been working on the ship. She wants to get back to them."

Kristen wraps her arm around me. "I'm sorry, Alli." She pulls me into her. "But we'll go parasailing and take your mind off it!"

She says, like that's some kind of consolation?

I grimace even though I don't mean to.

Kristen frowns a little. "Oh come on, Alli!" She says. "It will be fun as long as you get the stick out of your ass."

I roll my eyes. "I think I'm allowed to have a stick in my ass right about now." I mutter.

Kristen starts dragging me towards the bus for the excursions with a handful of other random people. We get onto the bus and Kristen sits next to me while Kevin takes the seat in front of us, still absorbed in whatever is on his phone.

"Have you heard from Louis?" Kristen asks, but the question feels leading.

"Maybe." I hedge. "Why do you ask?"

Kristen shrugs. "Just curious. I know he's been texting me asking about you."

I blink a little. "He texts you?"

She nods. "He's worried about you, Alli."

"I'm fine." I insist.

She doesn't challenge it.

The rest of the bus fills in with people all going to one of the nearby docks for different activities. A couple sits down behind us, chatting softly about the different things they have planned for the day.

"But you never answered my question." Kristen pushes. "Have you heard from him?"

I sigh and run a hand through my hair. "It seems like you already know the answer to that question, Kris, so I don't know why you're asking."

She shrugs. "I'm just curious what he said."

I fold my arms over my chest, annoyed by this entire conversation. "He sent a shirt-less pick and said he missed me."

"He does miss you, Alli." Kristen says. "He made a mistake, are you going to hold it against him forever?"

I put my hand on my chin. "Hmm, let me think about that for a second?" I pause as if looking off in thought even though I already know the answer. "Umm, yes. I intend to hold it against him forever."

"Well, you can do that and still love some-one." Kristen muttered. "I know you still love him, Alli. That's why you even opened the message he sent you in the first place."

I groan. "Do we have to talk about this?"

"You've been avoiding talking about him for months. So yes," Kristen takes a breath, "We do need to talk about this because you're never going to feel better if you don't talk about it."

"I don't want to feel better." I scoff. "I want him to take a long walk off a short cliff and never call me again."

"Prove it." Kristen says, taking my phone from me. "Block him."

I take the phone back from her, "I have nothing to prove." I shove it into my purse. "I will block him when I'm ready and in the meantime–"

She cuts me off. "In the meantime you'll stalk his socials like it's your job and pretend he never existed when anyone tries to bring him up with you?"

I chew on my lip.

"See, this is why we have to talk about him." Kristen is about to say something else when the doors of the bus close and it lurches forwards. I do my best to keep steady in my seat, but grimace at the way we are just about slammed into the seats in front of us.

"I get you're just trying to help, but I am going to heal my way and I need space and time to do that." I tell her, pulling a ponytail holder out of my purse and pulling my hair up into a messy bun because it's so blasted hot I no longer care if people see the hickeys. "I don't know if Louis and I will ever be back together again, but right now I have someone else making me happy and I want to focus on that."

"Speaking of Kai..." She nods at the hick-eys. "Looks like you two had fun while I've been stuck with this one." She huffs, pointing at Kevin.

I fight the urge to remind her that she chose to be stuck with him and that divorce is always an option, but in the end I just sigh and move on. "Yeah." I chuckle. "She spent the night."

"You've never been with a woman, what was that like?" Kristen asks, literally on the edge of her seat like she's trying not to fall off of it.

"Different," I shrug, "But in a good way."

Kristen looks at me like she's waiting for me to say more, when I don't she prompts me, "And?"

I debate how much information I want to give her let alone how much I want to tell a bus full of strangers who might be listening. "I don't want to have this conversation."

Kristen sighs. "I'm starting to feel like you just don't want to talk to me." She huffs, crossing her arms over her chest.

"No, I just don't want to talk about my nonexistent love life." I counter. "Can't we talk about what you've been up to the past few days?"

She pulls what looks like a water bottle out of her bag but sure as fuck doesn't smell like it. Probably vodka, although the bottle is blue so it could be anything. We did order a lot of vodka ahead of time to be stocked in our rooms though. "Oh god, can we not?" She chuckles as I look at her incredulously and she concedes. "Okay, I see your point."

"Great, then we can talk about something else." I suggest again, "Like why we picked parasailing of all the fucking things."

"Because it will be fun!" Kristen argued. "Parasailing will give us an amazing view of the island and it's mostly safe."

"Mostly." I mutter, stealing the water bottle from her and drinking some of it down.

Yup, definitely not water.

Parasailing was a fucking nightmare.

Kristen and Kevin started arguing the second we got on the boat and that meant I got shuffled in between the two of them when we got into the harnesses. We spent the entire time up in the air with Kristen annoyed that Kevin was being absent and Kevin arguing that he was here wasn't he and that should count for something. I was just trying not to throw up from the heights and the motion and the fact that I had finished half the bottle of what I learned was in fact vodka.

We got back to the ship in one very un-peaceful piece. Kristen and Kevin are on the make up sex part of their endless cycle of arguing and that means that I get some time alone to go to the Smoke Show before dinner.

I try not to hurry my pace as I walk through the hallways, I did change out of my swimsuit from parasailing but my hair is still sopping wet. I pull open the door to the Smoke Show and before I even get a chance to walk into the room I see Kai behind the counter chatting with a woman who seems to also be bartending.

I freeze a little as I see Kai reach out and rest a hand on the woman's arm with a smile, both of them giggling at something that I won't be asking about because I turn heel and just about run from the damned bar.

There is no call behind me so I don't think Kai saw me but I also don't know if she would go after me if she did.

I know I'm overreacting just a little bit. She has her own life and she doesn't owe me any kind of explanation for the friends she keeps or the life she lives outside of me. We aren't together and I don't have any kind of room to tell her not to laugh and rub the arm of her coworker. But something about seeing her with another woman just brought back flashbacks of finding Louis with Missy.

Kai isn't Louis.

I know that. It's not fair to put Louis's sins on Kai's head, but in this moment all I want to do is go back to my room and cry.

I make it into the elevator before my phone goes off. I expect it to be Kai, asking me how parasailing went or Kristen, telling me she wants to hang out because Kevin is annoying her again, but it's not.

It's Louis.

I freeze just in time for the elevator door to open and I almost miss getting out entirely because I'm too busy staring down at my damned phone. I manage to snap out of my trance and head out onto my floor. As I walk past Kristen and Kevin's room, I can notably hear them fucking and hard too by the screams. I'm surprised they haven't had a noise complaint yet.

I swipe my key card and push inside my own room, tossing my phone onto the bed so I don't open the snap.

Don't. Open. The. Snap.

My steps eat up the carpeting as I pace back and forth trying to calm myself down. Trying to remind myself that the best thing to do is to just not open it, delete it, and move on with my life, but if I'm being honest that hasn't stopped me any of the other times.

After a solid five minutes of thumping back and forth across the floor in a way that assuredly is pissing off my downstairs neighbor, I finally give in and launch myself onto my bed to check my phone.

I slide the screen open and assume it's going to be a picture of him again but it's not this one is a video. I open the video and the first few seconds play on a loop.

"Liss," He slurs my name like he's been drinking, "I'm so fucking sorry." He sniffles into the phone. "I know you de–" The snap cuts off and loops but I press down on my phone to move to the next video, "–serve better than me, I know that. But Kristen told me you met someone and–" I press down again, "–I can't imagine the thought of you with him. Please baby. Please forgive me. Please call me." The snap loops again but this time I don't press down.

I let the video go a few more times, tears welling up in my eyes from him being so vulnerable. It only took ten years, a break up, and him getting hammered to do it, but still it counts for something. It counts for trying.

I press down on the screen and the video goes away.

Day Seven

K ai has sent me five snaps and I haven't responded to a single one of them. I never snapped back Louis either. I spent last night curled up in my bed eating pasta I ordered from room service and watching whatever was on the TV in the room that I've already forgotten about now.

We have another day at sea before we actually dock anywhere again. Kristen and Kevin have been spending that day together which means I could go to the Smoke Show and see Kai by myself but a part of me is scared I'll see the other woman she was with yesterday.

Wow, I sound ridiculous.

I roll over on my bed and stare at the ceiling, trying not to think about Kai or Louis or how my best friend is assuredly in the other room getting rail by a jackass.

I haven't even been reading. I tried but I couldn't get my mind to focus on the words on the page, they all just started swirling around like mush. Then I tried skimming and none of it made any sort of sense, so I just threw my kindle back in my suitcase and gave up.

A knock sounds on the outside of my door and I'm sure it's Kristen about to come bug me to go sit by the pool or something because she's over Kevin again. I just roll over and ignore the sound, not really feeling like talking to anyone.

"Alli!" Kai calls through the door.

I jerk upright. "Yeah?" I call back.

"Open the door!" She yells. "I only have a few minutes!"

I rush over to it and undo the lock before yanking it open. "Hi." I say softly.

She scoffs at me. "You've been dodging my messages since last night and all you can say is hi?" She's wearing her work uniform and doesn't make any move to come in. When I don't say anything else she says, "I'm on my thirty, I only have a few minutes before I have to get back downstairs because of how long it takes to get across this blasted boat. Why are you avoiding me?"

"I'm not." I run a hand through my hair and lean against the door. "I've just been busy."

Kai pulls her phone out and flips it around to show me the time, "It's four p.m." She insists. "We've been at sea all day and you haven't snapped me or messaged me or come to see me since I left your room yesterday morning."

"I–"

"What was it? Just wanted to try hooking up with a girl and now that you've had your big lesbian experience you don't give a crap about me anymore?" Kai hisses.

"No!" I glance around the hallway nervously before sighing and ushering her into the room. "Just come in."

She scoffs, "Why because you're ashamed of me?"

"Because you're yelling in the hallway at your job and I don't want you to get in trouble." I mutter. "Just get inside."

Kai pushes past me, clearly annoyed, but apparently also seeing my logic.

I let the door close behind us and it just about slams because I just drop it instead of making sure it closes softly. "Look," I tell her, coming further into the room and moving to sit down on the bed, "It's not you."

"'It's me?'" She finishes. "Alli that is the most cliche break up line there fucking is."

"I'm not breaking up with you." I insist. "I didn't even know if we were together-"

"We're not!" Kai sneers.

I nod, "Right, so then why are you banging down my door after a day of not seeing me?"

Kai freezes. "I..." She stumbles over her words. "Why are you such a bitch?" She turns to leave but I stand up and block the doorway in what is definitely not one of my finest moments. Kai crosses her arms over her chest, but she doesn't try to push past me.

"I care about you, Kai." I whisper, "But we both know this isn't going to last. I have my own life and you do too."

She runs a hand through her hair.

"I still want to see you again while I'm here," I whisper, "If you'd be okay with that."

Kai chews on her lip. "I don't want you to ghost me again." She looks at me, her eyes soft and full of a sadness I know I can't do anything about.

"I can't promise that."

She nods. "I know."

A silence passes over the two of us that feels longer than it is. I don't know what to say to make this right but if I told her anything else it would be a lie. I can't promise I won't just disappear on her at the end of the cruise. I have to do what's best to protect myself and something I learned from Louis is that sometimes that's walking away.

Kai checks her phone. "Oh shit, I've gotta go."

I move out of the way and she walks to the door, looking back at me before she leaves. "Am I going to see you again?" I ask her.

She shrugs. "You know where to find me." Then she leaves, the door closing behind her with a heavy thud.

It's formal night in the dining room and of course Kristen loves that kind of shit. She's spent the last hour treating me like her personal dress up doll, doing my make up and hair and insisting I wear the full length dress instead of the mid length one.

The dress is the bridesmaid one I wore to her wedding, but it works for formal events too. It's a burnt orange that complements my skin tone better than I was expecting when Kristen picked them out. The dress has a v-neck and flowing skirt with a slit up the front and a similar sleeve that covers just the upper arm.

Kristen, of course, has multiple full length dresses to choose from both in her closet back home and packed into her suitcase now. She ended up in a light blue one that complements her hair perfectly and has little white flowers all over the sheer overskirt.

She gave both of us a soft glam make up looks that matched with our dresses coloring and curls that were easily good enough to be in a movie.

Kevin was supposed to come too, but after him and Kristen spent five minutes arguing because he still wasn't dressed even though dinner was in ten minutes, she decided to just ditch him, dragging me along through the hallways beside her towards the dining room.

I run a hand through my curls as I take another bite of chocolate cake, our meal having been surprisingly peaceful without discussion of Kevin, or Louis, or Kai.

Kristen smiles happily into her tiramisu. "Want to get drinks after this?"

"Depends where you're trying to go." I mutter, taking the last bite of chocolate cake into my mouth. I sent Kai back a snap of the water to keep our snap streak alive but I haven't messaged her other than that. She sent a snap back too of the water from the window in the Smoke Show and no caption and we haven't communicated otherwise.

"I think you should talk to Kai." Kristen says.

I hadn't told her that Kai and I had talked and that it didn't go well. At least, I don't feel like that conversation went well. "I'm good." I mutter, taking a sip of my wine.

Kristen frowns in that way she does when I'm doing something annoying. "You're be–ing stubborn. You won't talk to Kai, you won't talk to Louis. You're almost thirty, Alli. You're never going to be happy if you can't communicate with your partner."

"Yeah, because you're the expert on that." The words slip from my lips before I have a chance to think better of them.

Kristen's eyes go wide. "Excuse me?"

I consider apologizing and telling her I take it back. I consider pretending I didn't say it and just getting up and walking away, but in the end I already dug this hole, might as well say what I think. "Kristen, you and Kevin have fought every day we've been here. Do you really have any kind of room to tell me that *I* don't know how to communicate with a partner?"

She scoffs, crossing her arms over her chest annoyed as she takes a sip of her wine, but I don't let up.

"And by that token, are you even fucking happy?" I ask her. "You've spent four years with Kevin and I have never once heard you tell me a single good thing about that man other than that he's great in bed."

"I'm sorry that I've been confiding in you about the issues in my marriage because you're my best friend. Next time I'll just not talk about my problem. I'll just keep it all bottled up since apparently I can't go to you when I'm upset." She hisses.

I shake my head and try to lower my voice so we don't cause a scene. "Kristen, that's not what I'm saying. Of course you can always come to me with your issues, but you never come to me with the good things so it's hard for me to believe there are any."

"There are good things about him." She assures me like she thinks that will be the end of it, but I push.

"Then name one."

Kristen freezes. "I..." She trails off.

I don't interrupt her with an I told you so. I just let that hang in the air, giving her something to consider. She needs to truly think about her relationship and where it's going.

As if the universe wants to fuck me over, my phone, which is face up on the table, goes off with a snapchat from Louis.

"Answer it." Kristen demands.

I pick up the phone and hide it under the table in case he sent something inappropriate but it's not. It's just a picture of our dog. Alfonso has always liked Louis better and I knew that even though I hated Louis at the time, Alfonso was better with him than someone who was never home, but I miss him.

I flip the phone around and show Kristen the picture.

She smiles. "Awe." She swoons.

"Yeah." I whisper, staring down at my puppy on the couch of the new apartment that I don't recognize. His crinkling sharpei face scrunched and tilted as he looks into the camera. "I guess he's not all bad." I mutter softly.

Kristen nods. "Snap him back." She prompts.

"I..." I stumble over my words, but Kristen takes the phone from me and moves over to my side of the booth we are in.

She holds the camera back away from us and takes a picture in which I'm definite-ly not smiling, but she is cheesing for the camera. She doesn't send it, instead passing me the phone back to make the decision for myself.

I click the little caption box and my fingers fly over the screen faster than I have time to process what I'm typing, *"I wish you were here."* Then I hit send and the picture goes off into the ether.

Day Eight

This beach is the only bout of peace I've had over the last couple days. I decided to spend the day alone and lose out on the money from the guided hike we were supposed to do. I just couldn't take anymore of Kristen and Kevin's screaming matches.

They did go on the hike though and Kristen has been messaging me the entire fucking time telling me what a fucktard her husband is as if I don't already know that. She still hasn't managed to think of one nice thing to say about him and I can tell she has been trying.

The sun soaks into my skin, warming me through to my core. I didn't bother to try and grab one of the cabanas or chairs that were available, I just want to lay in the sand, needing the grounding feeling of actually touching the earth after being trapped on the moving water. I have a towel to dry off with if I go into the ocean, but I didn't bother laying one out, choosing instead to scorch myself on the hot beach.

It's fairly packed, likely because I didn't go far from the ship, but I don't really mind the noise or the people. I have enough room for myself, that's all I need.

I check my phone, waiting to see if Louis has snapped me again. We started talking after I sent the picture, nothing too deep just stuff like, *how have you been? Still at the same job? How's the cruise?* Little things to get back on comfortable speaking term, but it's been nice.

He hasn't sent anything flirtatious or asked me about Kai. I still don't think he even knows that Kai is a woman and I honestly don't know if I should even bother telling him. Whatever this is between me and Kai, it's been fun but I don't know if I have it in me to deal with the heartbreak of losing her if I let myself get more attached.

She's been snapping me too and I did send her a picture of myself in my bikini at the beach to which she replied with a picture of her bar well and the caption, *"Hot."* But we haven't talked since then.

I know I should go see her.

I don't like the way we left things, but now that Louis and I are actually talking again... I know him and I aren't together, but it would feel like I was betraying him in some way.

Louis sends me another snap. It's a picture of him at the gym winking in the mirror. *"How's the beach, princess?"*

I chew on my lip and flip over onto my back. I take a selfie from above of just my body, that I can barely fucking see because of the sun, and the second I hit send I think better of that. First of all, terrible fucking angle. Secondly, the whole sending a sexy picture to my ex fiance thing. I mean given I was clothed, but that clothing is skimpy at best and what if he thinks I want something from him back.

Do I want something from him back?

I roll back onto my stomach and stare at the little icon through my sunglasses, or try to with the glare, waiting for him to open it. When he finally does I can feel myself having heart palpitations that I would like to believe are just from the heat but I've been plenty hydrated and it's honestly not that bad out today.

Louis doesn't send back a picture but he starts typing.

I stare down at the thing that indicates he's typing waiting for the message to come through but then it goes away. My stomach lurches for a second before I see the typing start again, then stop again, then start again. He doesn't know how to respond...

But then he does.

"Hey there, babygirl." Followed by a winking emoji.

I chew on my lip and debate what the best way to respond to this is. I mean he didn't really say anything. I could just not respond at all. I *should* just not respond at all. But then another message comes through.

"I've missed seeing your body."

I should shut this down. I should–

A snap comes through from Kai and the second it does I tab out of the conversation with Louis and go look at her message. The snap is a picture of her pouting behind the bar, *"I'm sorry about yesterday. Come see me?"*

"I'll be by later." I reply sending her a picture of me with the beach behind me and my tits pressed together from where I'm laying on my stomach.

I go back to the conversation with Louis and stare down at his little avatar knowing that he's sitting in the conversation staring at it too. I feel like a fucking harlot.

I shouldn't go see Kai later.

I shouldn't message Louis again.

I should spend the rest of the trip with Kristen trying to talk her into a divorce, not even six months after being married.

Kai snaps me back. *"You could be by now."* She suggests with a smirk on her face in the photo. The caption below that one read, *"There's lots of beaches."*

I chuckle a little. I really want to go see her.

I swap back to the conversation with Louis but he's not sitting in the chat anymore when I get back to it. I frown a little before reminding myself it's not fair to just expect him to wait around for me, but then just how deep that could go hits me.

What if *he* meets someone else?

It's not fair to expect him to keep waiting for me and clearly he's not going to wait forever. What if I miss my chance?

"I've missed seeing your body too." I reply back to Louis.

His reply is instant, *"Would you like to?"*

My fingers fly across the keyboard before I have a chance to think better of it. *"Yes."*

He opens it and tabs out of our conversation.

I turn off my phone, knowing he's going to take a minute because he'll have to get somewhere private. I flip onto my back and shut my eyes, soaking in the beautiful sunny day. If it wasn't for my racing mind, my asshole of an ex fiance, and the hot bartender, it would be a perfect day.

I hear my phone go off but in an attempt to force myself to have self control, I don't immediately get it. After all of like ten damned seconds I say fuck it and grab the phone.

Self control is for the birds.

I sit upright and hunch over so I am shading my phone enough that I can see it. The picture of him is quick and rushed with his cock just barely hard, but definitely hard enough that I can tell he was playing with it a moment prior. There's a blur to the edges of the photo like he was moving when it was taken. It's from a downwards angle in what seems to be a changing room. My eyes can't stop staring at his abs.

I don't know how much time passes as I stare down at the photo that I'm forcing myself not to lick and the only reason I'm not is because I'm in fucking public. Louis's workouts have done him good, he was hot before but now? Damn.

Eventually I do click out of the photo and force myself to try and come up with something eloquent to say. My fingers type out a few different options.

You're an exquisite specimen of the human physique.

Your body is like something out of a renaissance painting.

You should consider modeling for porn.
Hot.

I end up erasing all of those and send back a picture of myself again with the genuine smile that's on my face. *"I've missed you."*

He jumps back into messages. *"Enough that you're not going to go sleep with that guy again?"* Louis asks. I can't tell if it's malicious or not since it's just a message but it's coming across as more like he is just being protective.

"There is no guy." I reply but before he has a chance to say anything else, I type quickly, *"The person I met on the ship is a woman."*

"Is that why you left me?" He asks.

I roll my eyes and fucking hard too. *"No, I left you because you cheated on me, you dick, but thanks for the reminder."*

I close out of the chat with him and push to my feet in the sand. I dust myself off as best as I can before putting back on my cover up and storming away from the beach.

Fuck him. I'm going to see Kai.

I changed into that sundress I wore on the first day, having had a chance to use the washers yesterday, and walk into the Smoke Show. I still have sand stuck in every damned crevice of my body, but at least from a distance I look hot.

Kai is moping, wiping down the counter of the bartop until she turns her head to see me and a smile spreads across her face. "Welcome in." She says like I'm just any other patron but the second I make my way over to the table I've sat at the last few times

I've been in here she came to sit down across from me.

"Hi." I smile at her. "How's work?"

Kai shrugs. "Boring." She uses the rag she's still holding to wipe down the table in front of me like she's trying to pretend she's working even though she's sitting down, but neither Beau nor the other girl are behind the bar and none of the other cruise goers seem to mind. "How was the beach?"

"Beautiful." I smile, "But nothing compared to you." I run a hand through my hair and chuckle, "Is that too cheesy?"

Kai chuckles, "I like cheesy."

A silence stretches between the two of us as we both try to figure out what to say in this situation. What do you say to your hook up after spending all day talking with your ex?

Not that. Definitely not that.

Kai and I turn our attention out the window to the waves that are cresting across the horizon and dancing out into the ocean. "How was parasailing?" She asks.

"Fucking awful." I huff. "I got stuck between the two bickersons in the harness and I was drunk off my ass.

Kai laughs, "Oh no!" She cries. "That sounds awful."

"It was." I nod. "That's half the reason I skipped out on the excursion today. I didn't want to deal with their arguing."

"What do you have planned for tomorrow?"

"Snorkeling." I answer. "Which at least Kristen and Kevin aren't going to. I was supposed to go with my fiance but..."

"You're engaged?" Kai jumps back a little.

I shake my head. "Not anymore."

"Oh..." She whispers. "I'm sorry."

"This was... this was supposed to be my honeymoon." I huff out a nervous laugh.

Kai sets down her towel and stands up. She comes over next to me and hugs me. "I'm so so sorry, Alli." She whispers into my forehead.

I breathe in her soft scent and try to calm myself down before I start all out sobbing in the middle of this bar, but it's not really working. "Fuck." I whisper, wiping the tears away from my eyes. "Sorry."

She tilts my head up to look at her, "You don't have to be sorry, Alli." She rubs the back of my head gently with her hand.

"I should go." I whisper into her chest as the tears I'm trying to choke back stain her white shirt.

"No, Alli, stay." She says. "Let me get you a drink." She pulls me to my feet and drags me over to the bar top, this time pushing me down into one of the chairs before going behind the bar and starting to mix together something that looks a hell of a lot stronger than a watermelon mint mojito.

Kai pulls out a dab pen from her apron and tosses it at me. "Take a hit, but a small one, that shit is strong." She tells me as she keeps mixing together all sorts of random liquors, one set into a shot glass and the other into a taller glass.

I do as instructed, taking a baby hit of the pen.

"I didn't mean hit it like you're a middle schooler trying weed for the first time." She chuckles. "You can do better than that."

I glare at her softly before rolling my still bloodshot eyes and taking another hit of the dab pen, I don't go as hard as I would with Kristen's but I do hold longer than I did last time before passing it back to her.

"There you go." She smiles before passing me a layered shot with a yellowish liquor on the bottom and a creamy looking one on top. "That is a buttery nipple."

My eyes go wide as I choke on a laugh. "A what?"

"Just drink it, it's really fucking good, I promise." Kai pushes the drink a little closer to me. I shoot it back and Kai bursts out laughing. "You're supposed to sip it."

I huff. "How was I supposed to know that?"

She's still working through a fit of laughter as she says, "I mean, I guess I should have told you, but I just assumed you wouldn't shoot it." Kai takes a breath like she's trying to settle herself as she passes me the tall glass. "Don't shoot this one."

I level her with a look. "Yes, because that was what I was planning to do." I mutter.

Kai shrugs. "I never know with you."

I take a sip of this one and chuckle, "A long island?"

Kai nods. "Best drink for a broken heart."

"Because it's full of liquor and almost nothing else?" I ask her.

"I mean yeah, maybe." She smirks. "But I've never seen a broken heart that I couldn't cure with a long island and some magic."

"Magic?" I ask her.

She nods. "Maybe later I'll pull out my wand and rabbit."

Day Nine

Snorkeling went well but being the only one who was by myself on the excursion meant spending the entire time with the guides or in my head, thinking about Kai and Louis. All I wanted to do was get back to the Smoke Show or the boat so I could snap one of them, either of them.

I'm about to leave my room to go see her when a knock sounds outside my door. "One second!" I call as I pull my crop top over my head. I walk to the door and as I open it I see Kristen.

Her brown eyes are red and bloodshot as she wipes away tears that are clearly recent from the way they are still soaking her face. I pull her into a hug without even thinking about it and as I do I take a step out of my room and the door slams shut... without my key card.

Shit.

I can deal with that problem in a minute, right now I'm more concerned with Kristen.

She sobs into my shoulder, her whole body shaking from the way she's crying as the door to the room beside us opens and I see Kevin sneak past us like he's ashamed of himself. He fucking should be his wife is crying and he's fucking off to god knows where.

"Can I come in?" Kristen asks against my shoulder.

"I'd say yes." I huff a chuckle, "But... I kinda just locked myself out of my room." As I pull back from Kristen I see her eyes are wide.

"You did what?"

"It wasn't on purpose!" I defend. "When I stepped out to give you a hug the door shut and... Yeah, I'm gonna have to go talk to guest services to get another key."

Kristen just stares at me for a second before she starts bursting out laughing. "You locked yourself out of your room." She chuckles.

I sigh. "I blame you."

She shrugs. "I'm sure you do but you still were the one who did it."

"Yeah." I run a hand through my hair. "Are you coming with me or...?"

Kristen nods. "Yeah, I'll come with."

As we start down the hallway I notice that Kevin is already long gone like he just about ran from the two of us. He's not even outside the elevators so he must have caught one before we got there.

We climb into the elevator and I hit the button for the fourth floor since that's where the sign said guest services was. There's a silence that passes between the two of us and I don't know if she wants to talk about whatever happened or if she just wants to leave it alone.

"Are you okay?" I ask.

"No." She turns around and fixes her hair in the mirror in the elevator. "But I will be."

She smiles softly, more at herself than at me. "Kevin's a douche."

I nod. "Yeah." I try to say it like I haven't known that for years, but it definitely comes off like I had said *I told you so.*

Kristen huffs. "I would be mad that you're a know it all if you weren't just trying to protect me from myself." She mutters.

"Sorry." I run a hand through my hair as the elevator doors open and she heads towards the main portion of the ship where most of the shops and things are.

"Don't be." Kristen shrugs. "I'm sorry I didn't listen to you." There's a soft resignation there that she hasn't said yet, one I won't ask her about but I know she's feeling.

"Where was Kevin going?" I ask as we walk through the boat.

She scoffs. "Fuck if I know, or care." She says the last part softly. "He's probably off to waste more of my money at the casino again playing the stupid games."

Kristen did fairly well for herself and Kevin had always seemed to gravitate towards that more than her. I'm not surprised he's using this opportunity to go max out his credit card on whatever bullshit game that's probably not all that different from the free ones he could play on his phone.

I want to ask her if she's finally done with him, but I know she'll tell me when she's ready. If I ask too soon she might get defensive over her marriage and back slide right back into his arms.

We get to guest services and the random woman gets us a new key, our conversation fairly quick and benign just long enough to get the new one. They ask some basic security questions and for my room number and all that kind of random shit. It didn't end up being as much of a hassle as I thought it would be. I guess sometimes things can be a bigger deal in my head than they are in practice.

As Kristen and I head back towards the elevators I see the bartender that Kai had been friendly with in one of the other lounges on the ship, kissing a man over the bartop.

I don't stop or linger, I just keep walking like I didn't see anything, listening to Kristen talk about the last excursion we are going on. I think it's something with kayaking or canoeing or rafting or something like that but my mind is elsewhere.

Maybe the woman is straight. Maybe that touch on the arm was just that and I *way* overreacted. That or maybe the woman is bi and is super flirtatious with everyone and something is going on between her and Kai. And wow, that's a really presumptuous and awful thing for me to assume about someone whose name I don't even know.

"Alli." Kristen says as she presses the button for the elevator. "Are you even paying attention?"

"No." My eyes go wide and Kristen's do too, "I mean yeah. I just... sorry. I–"

"What is up with you?" Kristen hisses. "You haven't been yourself since we got on this fucking boat."

I chew on my lip, trying to tamp down my annoyance but I've just about had it. "Kristen, I haven't been myself for months." I snap at her and she stares at me like I've lost it. Maybe I have but I don't care. "My best fucking friend slept with someone else after ten damned years. That kind of shit changes a person. I'm *not* myself. You're right, but you've been too wrapped up in your marriage to notice."

I turn and storm off, deciding not to get onto the elevator with her.

"Where are you going?" She calls after me.

"To the Smoke Show!" I tell her. "Don't follow me."

Kai rubs my back as I tell her about what happened with Kristen and sob softly into my hands. "I'm so sorry, Alli." She kisses the top of my head. "I'm sure you guys will be okay though."

I shrug. "Probably." I mutter.

"You've been friends for your whole lives." Kai runs a hand through my hair and pulls me back to look at me. "You two will be fine. Sometimes friends fight. It's normal."

"It wasn't really even a fight though." I take a sip of the long island Kai made for me and know I must be in bad shape since she made it the second I walked through the door. "I just got mad and walked away."

"Has that never happened for you two be-fore?"

I shake my head. "No." I whisper.

"Happens with me and my sisters all the time." Kai shrugs. "We get mad at each other, don't talk for a few days and then come back like nothing ever happened." Kai moves to sit in the chair beside me at the bartop. "Maybe not the most healthy way of dealing with our anger, but it works for us."

"I don't think that's how Kristen and I work." I gulp down more of the long island.

"Maybe your relationship is changing." Kai suggested. "I mean, it sounds like she's always been the leader between the two of you, maybe you're just finding your own voice now that you're not following behind your ex fiance."

"Maybe." I chew on my lip.

"Excuse me." Someone says from behind us and Kai pushes up from the chair to go check on them.

Kai rubs my arm. "I'll be right back."

I nod into my drink and work the rest of it down, definitely having gone through it way faster than I should have. The buzzy feeling of the alcohol fills my head and I feel my phone go off in my pocket.

I grab it out and see Louis had sent me a snap.

Kai comes back behind the bar as I'm staring down at the screen. "Is that him?" She asks.

I nod again. "Yeah." I say, a tinge of sadness filling my voice as I try to pull my eyes away from the notification but can't.

"Are you going to get it?" She asks. There's no judgment in her voice, just a curiosity.

"I don't know if I should." I chew on the straw of my drink until Kai takes it away from me and starts making me a new one.

"What happened between the two of you?" She asks. "Why did you break up?"

I shake my head. "I don't really want to talk about it."

Kai pours the glass for the one man who had gotten her attention before coming back and finishing up my drink. There is a silence that passes between the two of us as she makes the drinks and I try to keep myself from reading too much into it. She passes me the new drink, this one a watermelon mint mojito.

"Try not to kill this one in five minutes or less." She chuckles and it feels like she's trying to be playful but I don't really love the implication that I guzzled the last one even if I did.

I let the glass sit in front of me as I turn my phone back off and slip it back into the pocket of my leggings. "How's work been?"

Kai chuckles. "You don't want to talk about that."

"I–"

She cuts me off. "Tell me about your ex."

I sigh. "What do you want to know?"

"I want to know why you broke up, but we can start with something smaller." Kai hums like she is trying to figure out what to ask. "How did you two meet?"

"Freshman orientation." I answer simply.

"Oh, come on," She whines, wiping down the bar like she's just looking for something to do with her hands more than trying to clean it. "You've gotta give me more than that."

"Do you really want to hear about Louis?" I ask her.

She chuckles. "Of course his name is Louis."

"What's that supposed to mean?" I ask, with a soft glare.

Kai shakes her head. "Nothing. Go on."

I sigh and take a sip of the mojito. "I was walking in late and there was a douchey frat guy who was a few years older who started harassing me. Louis was also late so when he saw me having trouble he wrapped his arm around me, called me babe, and escorted me inside. The frat dude took the hint and fucked off after that because my no wasn't enough but Louis's claim on me apparently was." I scoff at the memory.

"Still, sweet that he bailed you out." Kai smiles.

I nod into my drink. "Yeah, I guess."

"So what happened after you got inside?" She asks.

I chuckle and run a hand through my hair. "I haven't thought about that part in years." I chew on the straw as I have some more of the mojito. "Louis told me he was sorry about that guy and then went to walk away, but I stopped him and asked for his number because I appreciated the save. I texted him throughout all of orientation and didn't catch a word of what happened in it. We went on our first date a week later."

Kai swoons. "That's actually a way sweeter story than I was expecting."

I smile softly. "Yeah. Him and I have had some good memories."

"Tell me more?"

Day Ten

Kai pushes into my room like she owns the place, this time holding a small duffle bag that she tosses off to the side when she gets inside. "I brought some clothes and other shit since I ended up staying so long last time." She chuckles, running a hand through her hair nervously as the door shuts behind her.

Maybe I should find it presumptuous but just like with her not wearing a bra, it comes off more as confident. She knows what she wants and that's to spend the night. She's made that abundantly clear and doesn't mince words about it.

That was something Louis and I always struggled with was trying to be honest with each other about what we wanted. Having someone who's so the opposite is a nice change of pace.

"Make yourself at home." I smile as I move over to the couch and pour myself my second cup of coffee.

Kai collapses into me on the couch in a fashion that is overly dramatic and leans into my chest. "Can you make me a cup of coffee?" She asks.

I gladly pour her one; she's made me more than enough drinks, I can make her one coffee. I make sure to add tons of cream and sugar to hers like she likes and then I take a long sip out of mine before adding the same. It feels so personal that I know how she takes her coffee, will that always be something I remember from this trip? Will that knowledge fade away? Will my memory of her or her memory of me?

Kai smiles, "Thanks." She kisses me on the cheek softly, as her hand cups the side of my face like nothing has changed from the morning that we woke up next to each other.

I take a long sip of my coffee and it tastes exceptionally good. The coffee on this ship is surprisingly amazing for them probably making it in such large quantities. "How's your morning going?"

"Better now that I'm here." She smiles, snuggling into my chest as she takes a sip of her coffee and stares out at the water. "How about yours?"

I shrug. "It's okay." I have had no less than ten snaps from Louis since last night and I've opened all of them but responded to none. They have all been very sweet just checking in on me or sending pictures of Alfonso or himself or something equally benign, but I'm not ready to go back to that life yet.

It feels like a preview of where I'll find myself in about a week and I want to live in the now. I want to live in the moments I have with Kai before I go back home and find myself back in the same routine I've always been in.

Louis and I haven't gotten back together. We haven't made any decisions on anything, but I would be a fool not to see the writing on the wall. He's told me he wants to fix things while we've been talking and while I haven't told him my thoughts on that, I know that this Hawaiian getaway won't last forever.

"What's wrong?" Kai asks, turning up to look at me.

"I'm scared of what happens when I get back home." I answer honestly.

"Scared how he's going to react to you having been with someone else?" She clarifies.

I shake my head. "He already knows about that."

"Then how do you mean?"

"What if we just fall back into our old routine?" I ask her. "What if he becomes wrapped up in work and I stop trying because he's not listening and I find myself in another ten years on another cruise alone again because he slept with Missy Thompson *again*?" I sigh. "I just don't want history to repeat itself."

"Then don't let it." Kai says as though it's that simple. "Don't let him get too wrapped up in work. Don't stop trying. And for the love of god, don't book another cruise with him, Kristen, and Kevin."

I chuckle a little.

"The world keeps evolving," Kai smiles at me, "You can too." She takes a sip of her coffee and lets that hang in the air for a moment before adding, "You aren't the same person you were in that relationship, don't let old habits keep you from someone who you clearly care about."

"What about you?" I ask, before I can have a chance to think better about it.

She shrugs, "What about me, Alli?"

I chew on my lip. "What about whatever this is?"

Kai sits upright a little bit and looks at me with a sadness in her eyes. "Sometimes you meet the right person in the wrong place at the wrong time." She leans in and presses a gentle kiss to my face, one full of longing and a soft acceptance that this won't last. "The thing that makes life special is enjoying the time you have with someone. Nothing lasts forever, Alli. But in the time we do have, I want to enjoy it with you."

I press a kiss to her lips. "Come home with me." I whisper.

She shakes her head. "You know I can't do that."

"I'll stay with you?" I ask.

She shakes her head again. "You know that won't work." Tears form in the corners of her eyes. "Don't do this, Alli. Don't make this harder than it has to be or more than this is. This was a fun hook up. A great vacation romance. A beautiful experience for you where you finally got to try something you've always wanted and I met someone who I'll never forget. But we can't live in denial about what this is."

"What if we did?" I ask softly.

She chuckles. "What do you mean?"

"What if we pretend just for a little while that this could be more than it is? What if we daydream about the life we would create together and the way we would drop our kids off at soccer practice and go get hammered at book club with the other moms and gossip about that one bitch we don't like afterwards?"

Kai laughs. "Alli, that's crazy. Obviously we would enroll our children in something more elegant than soccer."

I smile at her. "Right, of course. Maybe swim team or volleyball."

Kai hums, "I don't like any sports where they could get hit with stuff. So no to volleyball, but I think swim team could work, but let's be honest, with your pension for singing, our kids would want to be theatre nerds."

"How many would we have?"

Kai takes a sip of her coffee, "Three, one of each."

I chuckle a little. "And we'd name them…" I chew on my lip. "Jamie. Oliver. And… Amelia."

Kai bursts out laughing. "We are not naming our daughter, Amelia."

"Fine, what are your name suggestions?" I ask.

Kai doesn't answer right away, seeming to think it over. She takes a long sip of her coffee before sitting upwards triumphantly, "I've got it!"

"Okay." I smile.

"Koa, River, and Ivy." She suggests.

"I like River." I concede.

She frowns. "That means you didn't like the rest."

"I liked them." I nod.

Kai sighs. "No, it's okay, we can keep thinking." She pulls out her phone and pulls up a baby naming website. "Meghan, Mia, Maya, Miranda. Why do all these start with M?"

"Definitely not something that starts with M." I groan.

"Right." Kai scrolls and starts looking at other names. "Are you carrying the babies or me? And who are we getting for the sperm donor? That's gonna change what we name them."

"I think we both carry one and then decide who it's safer for to carry the last one. If one of us has an obvious issue then it makes more sense for–"

She starts laughing.

I don't ask her why, I just start laughing too.

She lays her head on my chest as she stares out at the waves and sips at her coffee. "I like the idea of planning a life with you." She smiles.

I smile back. "Yeah, me too."

I just wish it was real.

Day Eleven

Kai pulls my shirt up and over my head. "Alli." She moans like my name belongs to her. Like I belong to her. She pushes to stand up and my hands reach out for her not wanting her to disappear so quickly, but she tsks. "I'm coming back." She promises.

She leaves me there naked on the bed as she goes and rifles through her duffle bag looking for something or maybe multiple somethings. Kai throws a set of handcuffs on the bed and I gasp a little bit. She just smirks at me and keeps going through her bag. After a couple more moments she pulls out a very intimidating looking wand that's definitely bigger than the one I have in my suitcase. She tosses it on the bed too and as she stands back up my eyes are fixed on the swell of her beautiful perfect ass.

"Ever used these before?" She asks, grabbing the fuzzy handcuffs and hanging them from her pointer finger.

I shake my head.

"Do you want to?" She asks.

I nod. "Yes." I whisper like it's the most scandalous thing I can even think of. My sex life has always been fairly vanilla. I was with my high school boyfriend and that wasn't anything more than a couple hook ups in the back of cars. Then there was Louis and while he had suggested some heavier things I had always been too scared to actually try any of them.

Maybe I've always been a little bit of a prude, but I had been raised in a community that wasn't very sex positive. I was already way outside of my comfort zone, I might as well jump into the deep end.

Kai smiles. "Wrists please." She demands.

I hold them out to her and she snaps the cuffs around them.

She runs a hand through my hair, "That's a good girl."

I blink a little trying to readjust to what she just said as a chill of anticipation runs down my spine. "I..."

"Is that too much?" She asks.

I shake my head. "No, I just... I've never really tried anything like this before." I admit softly.

"Do you want me to take them off?" She asks quickly.

I shake my head. "No. No, it's okay." I chew on my lip as I look down at the hand-cuffs on my wrists and the fuzzy pink covers. "I want to do this." I promise.

Kai nods. "If you change your mind just tell me to stop and I'll take them off right away." She assures me. "I want to make sure you're comfortable."

"I am." I chuckle, "Just nervous."

Kai leans down and presses a kiss to my lips from where she's standing off the bed. "No need for nerves." She pulls the cuffs to–wards her and shows me a little lever on the sides. "Press down on here and they release.

These aren't like police grade or anything crazy. They're just cheap ones I ordered online. You could probably break out of them with next to no effort." She runs her hand through my hair again before leaning in and kissing my cheek, "Besides, you're safe with me."

I nod and I believe her. "Okay."

"Do you want to keep going?" She asks.

"Yes." I smile.

"Lay down so you're comfortable." She smirks, "Well, as comfortable as you can get with the handcuffs."

I scoot into the middle of the bed and pull a pillow under my head. I take a breath and relax, trying to calm myself down. Everything is fine. Kai's got me. "I'm good."

"Good." She smiles, going to grab the vibrator. "Now put your hands above your head." She orders as she plugs the vibrator into the wall outlet.

I scooch down so that there is room for me to do that before readjusting the pillow and complying with her orders.

"Do you have a praise kink?" She asks.

I chew on my lip. "I don't know. I... I think so." I've always liked when Louis has told me in the past that I'm doing a good job or that he liked the way I was moving. I think that's what she's asking.

She chuckles a little. "Take a breath, Alli." She encourages and I follow her instructions. "You're doing great."

I smile a little at that.

"You're gonna be good for me aren't you?" She asks.

I nod. "Yes." I whisper.

"Good." She smiles as she brings the still vibrator down to my clit. She rubs the head of the wand up and down my slit and I buck underneath the touch with the anticipation even though her movements are nothing crazy.

I feel so bare with her standing over me in her t-shirt and panties when I have nothing on. It feels like another level of the power dynamic. I don't get to see her body yet and won't until she lets me. I don't get to touch her yet and won't until she decides otherwise.

I chew on my lip as I roll my hips trying to push further into her wand. I want to grind on it. I want more. I need more. "Please." I beg softly.

Kai smiles. "Take a breath, Alli." She orders again.

I do, but it's shaking and full of anticipation.

Kai chuckles. "Try again."

I inhale slower this time and as I do I feel some of the tension release from my body. "Okay." I whisper.

"More." She orders. "I won't turn it on until you actually relax."

I grumble, but try and shuffle myself in the bed so I feel less tense; it's not really working. I keep breathing and close my eyes so I can try and center myself. The waiting is killing me and the fact that it's over something I control is making me stress more which is the exact opposite of what I'm supposed to be doing.

"Fuck." I inhale through my nose and breathe out through my mouth over and over and over again.

"Let me see if I can help." She chuckles, climbing onto the bed beside me. Kai leans down and presses a kiss to my lips and I focus on that. I get lost in the feeling of her soft lips against mine. I get lost in the way she pulls my bottom lip between her teeth and bites down on it gently. I get lost as her hand that's not on the vibrator comes to rub circles around my stomach. "You're doing so good, Alli." She promises.

I nod and let myself believe her; that calms me more than anything else. I can feel some of the tension in my body dissipate and apparently it's enough for Kai because she switches the vibrator on.

Immediately, I jump.

Kai pulls the wand back away with a tsk. "Oh, Alli." She sighs like she's disappointed.

My eyes go wide a little as a frown spreads over my face. "Wait, I–"

She rubs my shoulder. "It's okay," She whispers, but it feels like she's taunting me, "Maybe you're just too nervous. I'll make you a deal."

I nod, already ready to accept whatever the hell it is before even hearing the offer.

"If you can make me moan, I'll turn the vibrator on and leave it on. No relaxing necessary." She smirks. "But you have to keep your hands on the top of your head while you try."

"Yes. Deal." I breathe out without even considering the verbiage or the ramifications or how the hell I'm supposed to make her moan without using my hands. It's fine, I'll figure it out.

Kai pulls her shirt up and over her head. "I'll help you out a little." She seems very fucking confident that she's going to win in the end of this little arrangement and I'd be lying if I said I wasn't nervous about that, but she said if I said stop she would stop so it's fine; I just have to relax and let what happens happen.

I struggle to maneuver, rolling onto my stomach and using all my core strength to pull my knees up and under myself.

Kai laughs as she watches me flounder, flopping around and doing my best to get myself upright. "This is more entertaining to watch than I was expecting." She smiles.

I glare at her a little but manage to get myself onto my knees. I tilt my head to the side and start to suck on her nipple. As I look up at her I can see her biting her lip forcing herself not to make any noise and realize how this is rigged against me. My tongue swirls around her puckered nipple and I wait for it to get nice and hard before I bite down on it.

Kai bucks under my touch and lets out a huff of a laugh but not a moan.

I kiss across her chest and move to her other nipple. I pull that one into my mouth next and flick my tongue back and forth across it doing the same thing on the other side but this time she gives less of a reaction.

Kai sighs. "Nice try." She goes to push me back down but I shake my head.

I lean up to whisper into her ear. "I'm not done yet." I smirk.

Kai chuckles. "Okay." She shrugs. "Take as long as you'd like." She smirks right back.

I trail my kisses down her jaw bone and to the side of her neck. As I leave kisses all over her neck she starts to take some deep breaths and I can tell I've got the right idea this time. I start sucking on the side of her neck and her whole body starts to shake.

Kai grits her teeth as the breath saws in and out of her. She's trembling under my lips but I don't stop sucking until she finally parts with it, her mouth dropping open as she gasps and lets out a very loud *moan*.

I pull away once the sound leaves her mouth, licking over the hickey gently to smooth it over.

"Okay," She smiles, "You win." Kai goes to push me down again and this time I let her. I fall backwards onto the bed, feeling extremely satisfied with myself.

Kai takes a moment to collect herself as I sit there in triumph. Once she's calmed herself back down she turns on the vibrator to the lowest setting and brings it down to my clit.

I moan immediately, having not been in a competition to suppress mine. I finally do relax into the bed and the handcuffs are barely noticeable at this point. They are there but they aren't.

I chew on my lip as Kai massages my clit with the wand. "Fuck." I moan, my eyes drifting into the back of my head with pleasure.

Maybe it's because hers is better or maybe it's because I've never had anyone else use a vibrator on me or maybe she's just that fucking good, but I've never had it feel like this before.

I smile, my head digging into the pillow as I squirm under her. "Kai." I moan.

Kai smiles. "Fuck, the way your body reacts is so beautiful, Alli." She runs her hand over my side and moves her fingers down to my entrance. Her fingers trace up and down my slit as she keeps the vibrator steady. She pushes her fingers inside a moment later and I can feel the way my pussy clenches around them.

She makes a come hither motion inside of me and my whole body bucks. "You have a perfect pussy." She purrs.

I let out a cry at her words as I can feel the orgasm starting to build inside of me. "I'm so close." I whisper.

Kai nods and keeps moving in the same way she was, keeping everything consistent as she brings me to the edge and then over it. She presses a kiss to my lips right as I scream out my orgasm and she swallows the sounds.

I keep crying out into her mouth while my whole body trembles underneath her, the pleasure taking hold of me in that way it does every time she's touched me. I will never forget this fucking trip so long as I live. I'll never forget her face or the way her hands felt.

I expect Kai to pull the wand back away now that my orgasm is over, but she doesn't. She starts moving the wand in little circles around my clit.

"One more for me, Alli." She smirks.

My eyes go wide. "I…" My words trail off as my brain hazes over, completely unable to think with how insane my orgasm just was. So stupidly I just nod. "Okay." I whisper even though I'm not sure my body can handle that.

My pussy aches from the orgasm I just had. The way the vibrator feels now is almost like a sting and I take deep breaths trying to get myself through the way she's manipulating my body.

"You're doing so good, Alli." She whispers.

Faster than I'd like I can feel my next orgasm starting to crest over the horizon and I take a deep breath and let it wash over me. It didn't take much from where I was to get me back there.

I let out a shaking breath and the second she pulls the vibrator wand away, I'm turning onto my side panting for dear life as I try to reconcile what just happened with the fact that it will probably never happen again.

Kai rubs my back, pulling me into her arms and helping me to relax into her. "You did so good, Alli." She praises as she takes off the handcuffs.

I smirk. "I'm not done yet." I promise, taking the handcuffs from her. "Your turn."

Day Twelve

I decided to skip rafting or kayaking or... canoeing... yeah, I still don't know which of those things it was actually supposed to be, but Kai and I have spent most of the day ordering room service and hiding under the covers. This is the last off day I'm going to have with her and I want to enjoy it. She could have come with to rafting or whatever, but we decided sex in the room was a better use of our time.

I collapse down onto the bed after my orgasm just hit me like a fuckin exorcism and Kai smiles brightly at me as she curls up beside me.

"Very good." She smiles. "How about another?"

She's about to lower the vibrator to my clit again when my phone starts ringing from across the room on the coffee table. I chew on my lip and she shrugs. "Get it, but just know I'm not done with you." Kai smirks.

"Are you sure?" I ask.

"Hurry up before it stops ringing." She demands.

I launch myself off the bed and after the phone, freezing a little when I see Louis's name flash across the screen. I flip it so she can see.

Kai whispers. "Answer it."

I don't have time to think over the decision, I slide the answer button across the screen before the regret can set in or the realization of exactly what's happening. "Hi." I whisper into the phone, not realizing how out of breath I sound until the word passes through my lips.

"Hey." He whispers back sadly.

There's a silence that passes between us as Kai stares at me expectantly like she's waiting for me to say something. Is he waiting for me to say something too?

"How are you doing?" I ask, but it comes across more as confused than as an actual question. I am confused though, I'm confused why he's calling me for the first time in nine months.

"I..." He seems to mull over what the right answer is. "I'm not great, Liss." He answers and the answer feels brutally honest. "This has been the worst year of my life."

I sit down on the couch, my eyes staring out the window as Kai comes up beside me.

"Put it on speaker." She mouths.

I glare at her a little because this feels very invasive, but I hit the speaker button anyways. "I'm sorry." I say to Louis.

"Is she there with you?" He asks.

I look at Kai. "Yeah." I admit softly.

"I... I should go." But he says it like he's looking for me to ask him to stay, like he's looking for me to choose him.

"Don't."

But it wasn't me who said that.

Kai takes the phone. "Don't go." She says again.

I look at her with wide eyes and Louis goes silent over the phone recognizing the other voice. "That's Kai." I whisper.

Louis sighs. "Yeah, I kinda figured. Although I didn't know her name until now. Hi, Kai." There's no malice in his voice as he says it. More of a curiosity and a longing.

"Louis." She smiles.

"Sorry to interrupt." He apologizes. "I should leave you alone. I can always talk to Liss when she gets back home."

Kai shakes her head. "No, I think you two should talk now. I think it would be good to have a third party to make sure your conversation stays on track."

He scoffs a little. "I'm not sure you're the best person for that."

"I'm not." She says. "But I'm the best you're going to get." She shrugs. "Why did you call Alli?"

"Kai." I hiss.

"No, it's fine." Louis sighs. "I called Liss to see if you were in her room." His honesty shocks me a little and I have to fight my jaw from dropping. "I guess I have my answer."

"Why else?" Kai pushes.

"I..." Louis huffs a laugh. "I don't know about this. Maybe I should just call Liss back later."

"No, I... I'd like to know the answer to the question," I push in a way I likely wouldn't have if I had been alone, but something about Kai gives me a confidence I never had before, I just hope it lasts.

There's a silence that passes as we wait for him to respond. I turn my head out to the waves watching them for one of the last times before I have to go back home. I don't want to go home to my empty house all alone.

"I love you, Liss." It's the first time I've heard him say that to me since we broke up and when he does the words come out of my mouth without a second thought.

"I love you too."

I look to Kai and she's smiling, but it doesn't reach her eyes. It's that kind of solemn smile with a bleak acceptance that this is the way things have to be, an acceptance that there will never be three children and swim practice and a life together like we want.

Kai rubs my shoulder gently.

"Please, baby." Louis whispers. "Can we fix this?"

My eyes are still fixed on Kai and she's nodding, telling me to say yes, telling me to do it, telling me to be with Louis even though she knows it will be hell for her.

She mutes the phone. "Say yes, Alli." She presses the button again.

"Yes." I whisper, more for her sake than mine. This is what she wants for me. This is what's best for everyone and I know that. "I want to fix this."

"I'm so fucking sorry." He apologizes. "What I did to you. It was the worst mistake of my life and I swear I will never hurt you like that again."

I nod.

Kai mutes the phone again. "Address the communication issues." She prompts. Then she hits the button again and the phone unmutes.

"You never told me when something was wrong." I say softly, but force some conviction into my voice. "You always let shit build up until you were picking fights with me or going out drinking with your buddies. If we get back together. I want to work on more than just the cheating."

"Yeah." He whispers. "Yes, of course. I'm so sorry, Liss."

"I don't want to hear that you're sorry." I tell him, not rudely, but honestly. "I want you to promise you'll do better. I want you to go to couples counseling like I've been asking you to for years and I want..." I take a deep breath. "I want to be stable enough to have kids."

Kai keeps rubbing at my back.

"I hear you, Liss." He promises. "I hear you and I want to give those things to you. I want to make this right. I'll do anything to make this right for you."

"I'll look for a couples counselor when I get back home." I smile softly, feeling rather accomplished in this conversation.

"I'll look too and send you some of the ones I see." Louis offers.

"Thank you." I whisper.

"Anything for you, Liss." He's quiet for a second before he asks. "Are we back together then?"

I chew on my lip. "I don't want to promise anything until I'm back home." I admit softly.

I can hear him nod through the phone. "Do what you need to do, Liss. I trust you and as long as you come back to me. That's all that matters." He says. "And Kai?"

"Yeah?" She asks.

"Thank you." He sounds genuine when he says it. "I don't think she would have ever found her way back to me if it wasn't for you."

I can see the tears rolling down Kai's face as she whispers back, "Just take care of her for me."

"I will." He promises. "I will."

"I should let you go." I tell him.

"Yeah." He replies. "I'll see you in a few days, Liss." Then he ends the phone call.

I set the phone down on the coffee table and look into Kai's eyes. There's a sense of heartbreak that passes between the two of us, both of us seeming to recognize that this can't go on anymore. That this has to be the end of whatever this was because once I get back home I'll be taken again.

"I should put on some clothes." She sniffles as she wipes away some of the tears from her eyes. I watch as she goes into her duffle bag and pulls out a new outfit. She puts it on and packs up the rest of her things that are scattered around the room. Kai throws them all in haphazardly and runs a hand through her hair. "I... I should go."

I nod. "Yeah." I whisper.

I don't want to. I want to tell her to stay, but I know she's right. I know she should go and I know that whatever this was. It's over.

Kai comes up to me and presses a kiss to my cheek. "Goodbye, Alli."

She heads towards the door and I stop her.

"Kai?"

She turns to look at me.

"Thank you." I whisper. "For every-thing."

She smiles. "I love you, Alli."

Then she walks out the door and out of my life without giving me a chance to say the same.

Day Thirteen

I've spent all day crying and trying to get my shit packed back into my suitcase since tomorrow is the last full day on the ship. Packing has been a bitch and when I was trying to I found one of Kai's t-shirts. I should have messaged her and told her, but I didn't. I packed it into my bag so I would always have a piece of her.

I didn't bother to go to the last island. I have no interest in seeing any more of Hawaii; I'm just ready to get back home to Louis. I chuck a couple more things into my makeup bag, questioning how everything fit so well on the way to the boat but nothing seems to be fitting together now. Like what the fuck is that bullshit?

Louis has messaged me a few times but I haven't answered any of them. Although I do jump every time my phone goes off hoping it's Kai, but it hasn't been. She's respected my wishes and she's let me have the space she knows I've needed. The space I wish I didn't need.

My mind keeps replaying all the moments I had with her, every beautiful second sitting and eating room service, laughing over jokes I can't remember now. The times she touched me and it felt like the world was tilting on its axis. When I first met her at the Smoke Show.

I want to go back. Just one more time I want to go back and see her, but I don't know if that's a good idea. I don't know if the best thing for either of us would be for me to walk in there.

Maybe closure just isn't real.

Sometimes you just never get that.

I'm fairly lost in my thoughts when a knock sounds on the door. I run to it, thinking maybe it's Kai, but when I open it, I see Kristen.

"Hi." I whisper.

Her and I haven't talked since we had that argument a couple days ago. I've been dodging her at dinner and neither of us have tried to call or see the other one.

"Hi." She whispers back. A moment passes before she asks, "Can I come in?" I look behind her and notice she's pulling her suitcase.

"Yeah." I nod, stepping aside to let her into the room.

Kristen walks in timidly in a way that's beyond out of character for her and sets the suitcase against the one wall before moving to sit down on the couch.

I let the door close and come over to sit crisscross on the bed. She doesn't say anything so I nod at the suitcase. "What happened?"

Kristen stares down at her feet. "Kevin and I broke up."

"How are you doing?" I ask.

She scoffs. "My marriage just imploded." She answered. "So... not great."

"I'm sorry, Kris." I offer.

She nods. "Me too." She takes a deep breath trying to settle herself. "Can I stay here for the rest of the trip?"

"Of course." I nod.

"Can you switch seats with Kevin on the plane so we don't have to sit next to each other?" She asks, chewing on her lip.

"As long as Kevin is okay with that." I answer.

"He is." She whispers.

"What happened?" I ask.

Kristen just keeps chewing on her lip. "He told me he hates me and that I was never good enough for him and that he only married me for my money." She said softly, the usual spark in her voice gone.

"He's a fucking asshole, Kristen." I tell her. "And if I wasn't worried about being thrown in whatever the cruise ship equivalent of jail is, I would go fucking deck him."

"Could you anyways?" She chuckles.

I smile a little. "If I see him." I nod. "You deserve better than him. You've always deserved better than him and I'm not just saying that because I'm your best friend. I'm saying that because it's true."

Kristen smiles back at me. "Thanks."

"Did you call and cancel the joint credit card yet?" I ask her.

She shakes her head. "No, but I should probably do that now."

I nod. "Yeah."

"Where's Kai?" Kristen asks.

I shrug. "Work probably, but I don't know."

"What do you mean?" She asks.

"I don't think we were ever actually together, but I do know that we definitely broke up." I take my glass of wine off the night-stand and take a sip of it. I've spent most of today drunk.

"I'm so sorry, Alli." Kristen says.

I nod. "Yeah. Me too."

Kristen and I skipped dinner. We stayed in the room finishing off the lasts of the bottles of wine we ordered, some of which she had stolen back from Kevin, which wasn't particularly hard considering that he hadn't even been in the room.

She laughs and leans her head against me as I tell her more about my time with Kai, spilling all the dirty details. "I can't believe you've never tried handcuffs before!"

I blush. "I mean, Louis has asked me too, but I've always been too nervous." I drink down another swig directly from the bottle of red. "I won't be scared now though." I smirk.

Kristen sits upright on the couch. "Are you?" Her eyes are wide. "Are you two getting back together?" She asks.

I shrug. "I don't know." I answer honestly.

She looks at me incredulously. "Alli."

"I think so." I admit.

She smiles, clapping as best she can around the bottle of wine. "I would say we should get some wine to celebrate," She raises her bottle, "But I'd say we've already more than done that."

I chuckle. "Yeah."

"You two were always good together." She smiles, sinking back down on the couch.

I lean into the headboard and shrug. "We've had our issues."

"No." Kristen counters. "Kevin and I have had our issues. You and Louis have always been good together. Remember when he proposed?"

I smile a little at that. "Yeah."

He had gotten Kristen to keep me out of our place the whole day so he could decorate it. When I got home the place was covered in rose pedals and real ones too, leading me all the way to our back yard. He had covered our gazebo in string lights and was down on one knee the second he saw me.

I kind of blacked out the rest and everything he said. The only thing I definitively remember is saying yes and that we got Italian food for dinner that night. The rest of the experience was a blur. It was like an insane high that I had never felt before and all I could think was that I was engaged and going to spend the rest of my days with the love of my life.

He is the love of my life.

But I will always love Kai too.

I start sobbing, all out dirty gross sobbing. I set the wine bottle down on the side table and pull a pillow into my face, crying into it.

Kristen comes up next to me, pulling me into a hug and whispering over and over again that everything is okay, but it's not.

Nothing will ever be okay again.

Kristen goes quiet and then she starts crying too. "I'm going to get divorced before I'm even thirty." She sobs into my shoulder.

"I'm never going to get to see her again." I cry into hers.

We spend a long time like this, both of us just losing it and ugly crying. I'm sure we've disturbed the neighbors next to us but honestly, I don't give a flying fuck. Today might be one of the worst days of both of our lives. It's our vacation and we can cry if we want to.

Eventually, I take a deep shuddering breath and pull back away from her. Kristen wipes her tears away with the blanket as we stare at each other both of us trying for the other one to keep some semblance of sanity.

"Whatever the fuck happens." I tell her. "I will always be grateful that I have you by my side." I smile at her.

Kristen smiles back. "Through hell or high water." She promises.

"Through hell or high water." I repeat back.

Kristen and I both sniffle as she grabs the wine off the side table, having left her bottle on the coffee table, and takes a long swig of it before passing it to me. "You should go see her."

I look at the clock. "I can't. It's almost midnight, the Smoke Show closes at eleven." I drink down some of the wine.

"Then text her." Kristen insists.

"What about Louis?" I ask.

She shrugs, taking the wine bottle back from me. "Fuck him." She hisses. "He cheated on you. You can go sleep with the hot bartender one more time."

I chuckle. "I'm not sure he'll see it that way."

"Then he can fuck right off." She's clearly drunk. "Look, I love you, dude. And I just think that... I just think you should go for it."

I take the wine from her. "I think you've had enough." I set the wine bottle on the side table again. "I'm not going to cheat on Louis."

"Are you two together?" She asks.

I chew on my lip. "Not really."

"Then it's not really cheating."

Day Fourteen

I know I shouldn't, I know it's a bad idea, but at the end of my last day on the ship I find myself walking to the Smoke Show. It's already a half hour past close but I'm hoping that Kai is still there and if she's not... if she's not I'll take it as a sign that I was just supposed to leave things as they were.

I get up to the doors and I see her in there alone wiping down the counter. The bar looks like it's mostly closed down and she's probably about to leave. I debate knocking on the door, I debate turning back around, but in the end it doesn't matter because she looks up from the bar and sees me.

Kai drops the rag and runs to the doors the second she sees me. She unlocks them and ushers me inside. There's no mincing words, there's no talking. She just pins me up against the door, locking it as she presses her lips to mine.

I kiss her too, my back against the glass doors as we both put everything we have into this kiss. Kai starts dragging me towards the bar with a very mischievous smirk on her face, our lips not breaking from our kiss. "I'm not supposed to go back there."

"It's my last day." She whispers into my lips. "Who fucking cares?"

I chuckle as she hits a switch and the lights in the bar go off. "You're so fucking hot." I whisper.

Kai lifts me up onto the bartop and pulls up the skirt on the dress I'm wearing, the same dress as the one I was wearing the first day we met. She yanks down my panties and I prop myself up as best as I can with my hands behind me. Her head slips between the two of my legs. She gives one long lick up my slit before making her way to the bundle of nerves at the top of my legs.

I moan, my head kicking back in pleasure as her tongue dances over my clit. I push myself into her, my eyes glancing around, scared we are going to get caught by someone, but we're at the back of the ship and there was no one around when I was walking back here.

She slips her fingers in between my pussy lips, fucking me softly with them over and over again as she eats me out.

I will never fucking tell Louis how much better at this she is than him. If he ever fucking asks I'll lie. I'll fucking lie through my teeth, but this is the best oral I've ever had in my fucking life.

"Kai." I moan loudly.

She shoots up to her feet and claps her mouth over mine quickly. Kai shushes me. "Just because it's my last day doesn't mean I want to get caught." She chuckles.

I blush fiercely. "Sorry." I whisper.

She shrugs. "It's fine, just try to keep it down." She tells me in hushed tones, her fingers never leaving my slit. She keeps fucking me with them and I can feel my body approaching the edge quicker than I want.

I push her away and she pulls the fingers out. "I think I actually owe you an orgasm." I smile at her.

Kai pushes up onto the bar and lays down across it. "Go ahead, Alli." She smirks. "Give me a reason to remember this bartop forever."

I climb onto my knees on the bar and unbutton her pants. With painstaking slowness, I pull them down her legs.

Kai is just about shaking with anticipation by the time I get to her panties. I don't pull them down though. I bite into them with my teeth and fucking rip. She gasps as the fabric leaves her body.

My teeth hurt a little because, ripping lace with nothing but teeth is not a fucking comfortable sensation and it kinda has that cottony feel and, I'm distracting myself.

I grab the panties with my hand and climb up her body. "Open." I whisper as I hover the panties over her mouth.

Kai chuckles but she opens her mouth as I asked her too and I shove the panties inside.

"To make sure we stay quiet." I smirk at her before pressing a kiss to her lips. I trail my kisses down to her neck, remembering that hickeys drive her wild. I latch onto the skin there and start to suck wanting to leave her one that will last long after I'm gone.

I keep sucking as she squirms underneath me and moans into the panties that are in her mouth. Kai's hands go to my hips pushing them down onto her and moving them so I am grinding against her stomach as I bite at her neck.

I keep moving even without her guidance and she moves her hands slowly from my hips up my body. She rests them on my breasts and I do my best to slip my arms out of my dress while simultaneously holding myself up. Somehow I manage to get my arms free and I pull the top of my dress down so it's bunched up around my waist.

I feel fucking exposed as I glance around the bar seeing the dark leather and wood under the glow of the moonlight. My attention doesn't depart from Kai long before I pull my lips away from her neck checking just how dark the hickey I left was.

It's damn near purple and I smile with a very accomplished feeling settling over me. "Good luck explaining that." I whisper as I kiss over to the other side of her neck and start to leave another one on the other side.

She's going to need a fuck ton of make up when she sees her family tomorrow. I make sure the next one I leave is just as fucking dark. As I start to kiss down her body over her shirt and down to between her legs I try to remind myself that I've received oral plenty of times and I know what feels good so assuredly I can figure this out.

I inhale deeply, taking in the decadent scent of her pussy as I shove my head between her legs and give one long slow lick all the way up her slit.

Kai shakes a little when I get to her clit and I flick my tongue back and forth over the bundle of nerves there. When she lets out a moan and just about flies off the bar, I know I'm doing something right. I keep licking the same way I was, trying to keep myself consistent with my movements, but honestly I've never done this before and my tongue is already starting to cramp even after just a few minutes.

Eating pussy, so much fucking harder than fingering a woman. Like I said, I don't think I give Louis enough credit, the man is trying his best. He's no Kai, but he's trying his best.

I keep licking up and down her clit and eventually I get to the point where I start massaging her with my hand because I'm struggling to keep my tongue moving in the way it needs to be.

So instead I kiss up her body and pull the panties back out of her mouth. I toss them down the bar and press a kiss to her lips as my hand works between her legs trying to bring her closer to the edge.

Kai moans into my lips, clearly trying to use me to muffle the sound as she glances around like she's just as scared we're going to get caught as I am. "Alli." She whispers. "Alli."

I nod, pulling back away from her lips.

"I love you." She pants out.

"I love you too, Kai." I press another kiss to her lips. "I will always love you. So long as I live I will love you."

"I'm so sorry, Alli." Her eyes fill with a sadness but I shush her.

"Don't." I tell her. "Don't do that. Don't think about that. Just focus on now. Focus on the time we have together."

Kai nods through her tears. "I love you, Alli." She says again.

I nod back. "I love you too, Kai." I repeat, my hand working between her legs as she gets closer and closer to the edge.

She gasps as she cries and it's clear she's getting close. I want to help her get there, but my eyes are starting to fill with tears too because now that I'm thinking about it, it's slapping me in the face just like it does every time.

Kai clears away my tears. "You're going to be okay, Alli." She promises. "You have a beautiful life on the other side of this."

I hush her. "I don't want to think about that." I tell her. "I want to think about you. I want to think about the life we would have together. I want to feel you finish on my fingers."

Kai nods and I can feel her body relax into my touch. She moans, starting to grind onto my hand as I kiss back down to her neck and suck back on the lighter of the two hickeys.

A few more moments pass by before Kai cries out in pleasure and my hand that's not between her legs jumps up to cover her mouth, trying to stop the two of us from getting in trouble for fucking in the middle of the bar.

Kai turns over onto her side the second the orgasm is done and starts panting trying to catch her breath. She takes maybe a minute before flipping us over so I was on my back on the bartop and she was on me. "One more for the road." She promises.

I nod as she slips her hand between my legs in my bunched up dress and starts to work me like I'm hers. A part of my heart will always be hers. A part of my soul will always be hers. A part of my body will always be hers.

I find the panties quickly stuffed into my own mouth as I make sounds that are way louder than advisable, but I don't stop. Hopefully I won't get banned from the cruise line if we do get caught.

I quickly approach the edge and feel myself in danger of falling off the fucking bar from the way I'm rattling underneath her. I do my best to try and calm myself down, try to slow down the orgasm that I know is going to wreck me; mind, body, and soul. But I can't. There's no stopping what Kai does to me.

My orgasm washes over me and I scream out in pleasure as I try my best to muffle the sound but I know that it's not. My body trembles and I inhale deeply through my nose and try to keep myself from passing out with just how strong that was.

I shoot upright, my breath sawing in and out of my lungs. I pull my legs into my chest as I start sobbing into my knees. I close my eyes and feel Kai's hand slip onto my back, rubbing soft circles around it.

"I love you, Alli." She presses a kiss to my forehead.

I pull my head out of my knees. "I love you too, Kai." I press a kiss to her lips, knowing it will be one of our last, both of us lean into it and I throw her arms around her shoulder, pulling her into me.

We separate and climb off the bar, leaving a mess all fucking over it. I glance at her and she looks at me two before we both burst out laughing.

I readjust my dress so that it's back into the right position and she fixes her clothing too. "Should we do something about that?" I ask.

Kai waves me off. "Nah." She shrugs. "It's my last day." She chuckles. "I couldn't give less of a fuck." I smile at her.

A silence passes between the two of us.

"This is the last time we are going to see each other." I whisper.

She nods. "Yeah."

The moment we had been dreading since this started was here. And I think in those moments when saying something is too hard. The best thing to do is to just say nothing at all.

Kai and I look between each other with everything hanging in the air, with the life we could have had if we had met under different circumstances. And in the end, instead of telling her how much I'll miss her or how I'm sorry this is ending. I just turn around and she does too.

I hear her steps retreating before I even take my first and when I turn back the kitchen door is swinging and she's gone.

A tear rolls down my face as I turn and walk out of the Smoke Show.

Acknowledgements

Thank you to you, the reader! I'm always grateful for anyone who picks up my books let alone finishes them and then reads the acknowledgements so thank you so much!

Thank you to my husband who always keeps me on task and keeps me going. It was because of his recommendation I took a break and started this story and because of that I now have Kai and Alli which is super fucking cool.

Thank you to my parents and my family who have always supported me. Without you I wouldn't be where I am today.

Thank you to my PA, Halla for everything she does. Halla is absolutely amazing and

I'm eternally grateful for how far I've been able to come because of her.

Thank you to Alli, oh and I'm sorry about the melancholy, I was really depressed.

Thank you to Kai, for taking care of Alli for me and giving her the experience she always dreamed of. And thank you to the person who gave me that experience too.

Thank you to all the authors who came before me and inspired my works. Nothing is ever original and I'm okay with that. Where have I heard that before?

As always, thank you to typos. Withoot you I would be nothing. You make me the author I am today and I love you.

Finally, I want to thank God, because God gave me this book, and I feel God in this Chili's tonight.

About the Author

I'm bad at talking about myself but can write a 500 page book about someone else. Do with that information what you will.

As a kid I dreamed of being an author. I took a creative writing class in high school then proceeded to go on with my life and do nothing with it. That was until one day I decided to open a silly little document and start writing a silly little story about a healer and two kings who were in love with her. That cute little pet project that I thought would just be scrapped ten chapters in turned into a full blown trilogy that I'm more proud of than I can even explain.

I've always been a dreamer and sometimes if you keep your head in the clouds long enough, you do actually touch the stars.

I got married in September of 2024 to my loving husband. We had been together 4 years at that point and he's always encouraged me to go after what I'm passionate in. Finding that person who helps you achieve is so important and it's the best quality trait I could ask for in a partner.

Thanks for spending your time to read this. I hope you're having a great day and please make sure to check out my works. There's always more coming out. I'm one of those people who always has to be working on something so I promise you I am.

Check Out My Other Works

<u>The Asher Series</u>
> Asher
>
> Burned
>
> Change

<u>A Literal Series Name</u>

A Cozy Airport Read

A Dark Romance Christmas

The Words We Put on Our Tombstones

The Siren and the Smoke Show

Check Out My Socials

Tiktok: @84Lele

    Tiktok Again: leanne.alyse

    Instagram: @the84Lele

    Twitter: @84Lele84Lele

    YouTube: @84Lele

www.ingramcontent.com/pod-product-compliance
Lightning Source LLC
Chambersburg PA
CBHW020114310726
48970CB00002B/629